THE USBORNE ILLUSTRATED
ATLAS *of* WORLD
HISTORY

LISA MILES

DESIGNED BY RUTH RUSSELL

MAPS BY JANOS MARFFY AND GUY SMITH

ILLUSTRATIONS BY PHILIP ARGENT AND JOHN LAWRENCE

COVER ILLUSTRATION BY JANOS MARFFY AND IAN JACKSON

CONSULTANTS
ANNE MILLARD, GRAHAM ROBERTS, GRAHAM TINGAY,
CHRISTOPHER SMITH AND JIM MORRIS

NOTE ON DATES

Some dates used in this book are marked either "BC" or "AD". BC means before the birth of Christ, which is taken as the year 0. AD means after his birth.

When dates appear with a "c." before them, this means that the date is not certain, but approximate. The "c." stands for *circa*, which is Latin for "about".

CONTENTS

THE EARTH BEGINS

Most scientists believe that the universe began with a huge explosion called the Big Bang, which took place between 10 and 20 billion years ago. The Big Bang produced immense clouds of gas and dust.

The Milky Way. This is the group of stars and planets, called a galaxy, that the Earth belongs to.

Planets revolve around stars. The Earth revolves around a star called the Sun.

THE SOLAR SYSTEM

Dust and gas from the Big Bang explosion slowly collected into balls which developed into stars and planets. A star called the Sun became the middle of our Solar System, with planets revolving around it. There are nine planets in our Solar System and Earth is the third nearest the Sun. All the planets are very different from one another. Those nearest the Sun, such as Venus and Mercury, are hot, heavy and made of rock. Those farther away, such as Jupiter and Saturn, are colder, lighter and made of ice and gas.

The Solar System formed from the gas and dust released during the Big Bang.

INSIDE THE EARTH

This diagram shows how the Earth was formed, 4,500 million years ago.

THE EARTH

At first, the Earth was probably a glowing ball of molten material. It took millions of years to cool and for a rocky crust to form. Many more millions of years passed before the atmosphere and oceans formed.

Scientists have tried to calculate the age of the Earth from rocks in space that have entered the Earth's atmosphere and hit the ground. These rocks, called meteorites, have been dated at around 4,500 million years, which is thought to be the age of Earth itself.

When in the Earth's atmosphere, meteorites are called meteors. They make a streak as they go.

Atmosphere. Gases escaped from the Earth to form a layer around the planet.

Crust. The outer layer solidified to form the Earth's rocky surface.

Inner core (solid metal). Heavy metals sank to the middle to become the core.

Mantle. Rock hardened around the core.

Outer core (liquid metal)

THE OCEANS

At first there were no oceans on Earth, because the planet was too hot. As the Earth cooled, gases cooled into water and the seas began to form. Volcanic eruptions poured out more gas and the seas increased in size to become oceans.

The first living things developed gradually, or evolved, in the oceans because it was too hot for life to exist on land. Over millions of years, more complex animals and plants evolved and some emerged from the water to live on land.

A volcano is an opening in the crust to the inside of the Earth. Molten rock and gases explode from it.

This early shark lived around 395 million years ago. Fish were the first animals that evolved with a backbone.

THE CONTINENTS

The Earth's surface is made up of large plates which move slowly, causing the continents to drift. This idea is called plate tectonics. Scientists believe that, around 300 million years ago, the continents were joined together in one big land mass. Scientists call this land mass Pangaea.

The continents then drifted very slowly apart to where they are today. The continents are still moving and in the future the world may look different again.

340 million years ago. The continents collide, forming one huge land mass, called Pangaea.

Around 100 million years ago. Pangaea has broken up into Gondwanaland and Laurasia.

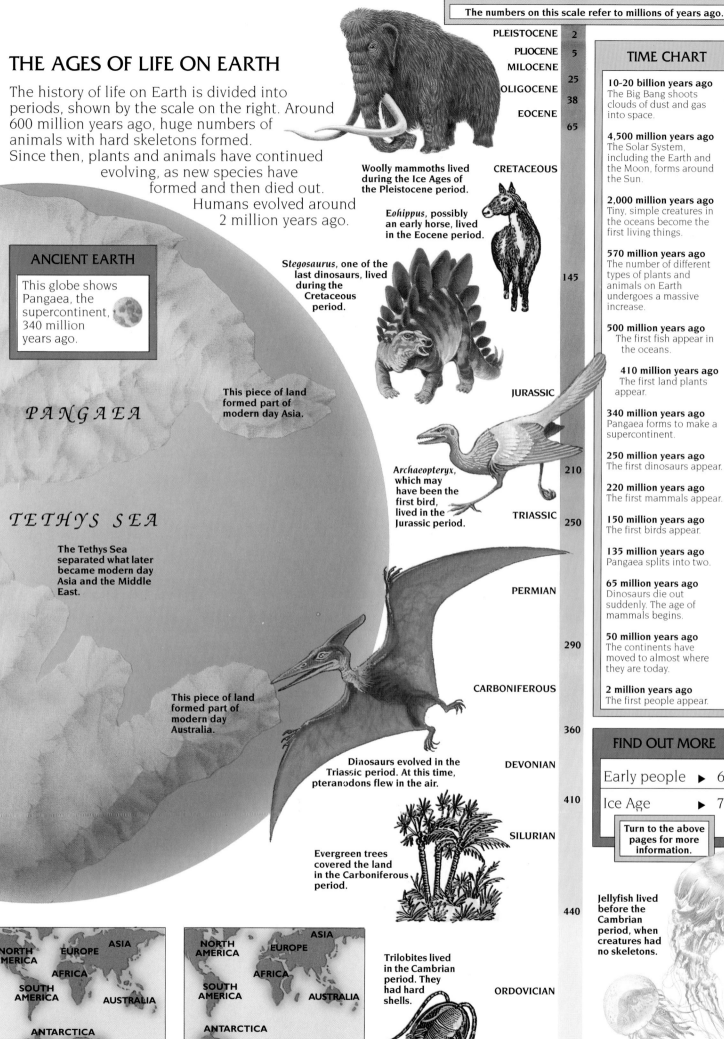

THE AGES OF LIFE ON EARTH

The history of life on Earth is divided into periods, shown by the scale on the right. Around 600 million years ago, huge numbers of animals with hard skeletons formed. Since then, plants and animals have continued evolving, as new species have formed and then died out. Humans evolved around 2 million years ago.

ANCIENT EARTH

This globe shows Pangaea, the supercontinent, 340 million years ago.

PANGAEA

This piece of land formed part of modern day Asia.

TETHYS SEA

The Tethys Sea separated what later became modern day Asia and the Middle East.

This piece of land formed part of modern day Australia.

Woolly mammoths lived during the Ice Ages of the Pleistocene period.

Eohippus, possibly an early horse, lived in the Eocene period.

Stegosaurus, one of the last dinosaurs, lived during the Cretaceous period.

Archaeopteryx, which may have been the first bird, lived in the Jurassic period.

Dinosaurs evolved in the Triassic period. At this time, pteranodons flew in the air.

Evergreen trees covered the land in the Carboniferous period.

Trilobites lived in the Cambrian period. They had hard shells.

Jellyfish lived before the Cambrian period, when creatures had no skeletons.

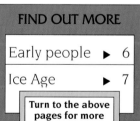

NORTH AMERICA **EUROPE** **ASIA** **AFRICA** **SOUTH AMERICA** **AUSTRALIA** **ANTARCTICA**

50 million years ago. By now, the continents have moved to almost where they are today.

NORTH AMERICA **EUROPE** **ASIA** **AFRICA** **SOUTH AMERICA** **AUSTRALIA** **ANTARCTICA**

50 million years in the future. No one is sure, but in the future the continents may move to the positions above.

The numbers on this scale refer to millions of years ago.	
PLEISTOCENE	2
PLIOCENE	5
MILOCENE	
	25
OLIGOCENE	38
EOCENE	
	65
CRETACEOUS	
	145
JURASSIC	
	210
TRIASSIC	
	250
PERMIAN	
	290
CARBONIFEROUS	
	360
DEVONIAN	
	410
SILURIAN	
	440
ORDOVICIAN	
	500
CAMBRIAN	

TIME CHART

10-20 billion years ago
The Big Bang shoots clouds of dust and gas into space.

4,500 million years ago
The Solar System, including the Earth and the Moon, forms around the Sun.

2,000 million years ago
Tiny, simple creatures in the oceans become the first living things.

570 million years ago
The number of different types of plants and animals on Earth undergoes a massive increase.

500 million years ago
The first fish appear in the oceans.

410 million years ago
The first land plants appear.

340 million years ago
Pangaea forms to make a supercontinent.

250 million years ago
The first dinosaurs appear.

220 million years ago
The first mammals appear.

150 million years ago
The first birds appear.

135 million years ago
Pangaea splits into two.

65 million years ago
Dinosaurs die out suddenly. The age of mammals begins.

50 million years ago
The continents have moved to almost where they are today.

2 million years ago
The first people appear.

FIND OUT MORE

Early people	▶	6
Ice Age	▶	7

Turn to the above pages for more information.

THE FIRST PEOPLE

Mary Leakey discovered many early human remains.

Most scientists think that humans are descended from the same ancestors as apes. It is thought that these ancestors came from Africa and that they may have lived 10 million years ago.

The chimpanzee, a great ape, is man's near relative.

THE SOUTHERN APES

Around 6 million years ago, the ape-like ancestors of men and apes began to change gradually, or evolve away from each other. By 4 million years ago, one group had developed into an early kind of near-human called *Australopithecus*. It was around 1m (3ft) tall and it stooped on two legs. This allowed it to carry things with its hands. Its name means "southern ape".

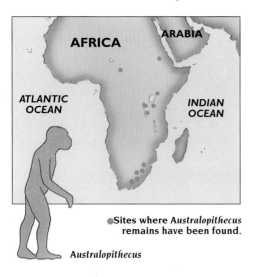

●Sites where *Australopithecus* remains have been found.

Australopithecus

THE FIRST HUMANS

The first true human evolved around 2.5 million years ago, when a different type of creature, or species, developed. This one had a bigger brain and was able to make simple objects from stone, pieces of antler, bone, leather and wood. It is known as *Homo habilis*, which means "handy man". The time in which he lived marks the start of what is called the Stone Age.

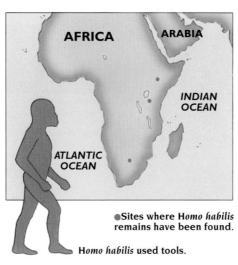

●Sites where *Homo habilis* remains have been found.

Homo habilis used tools.

UPRIGHT MAN

Around 1.7 million years ago, a new species called *Homo erectus* (meaning "upright man") developed. It made large shelters from twigs and branches and knew how to use fire, though not how to create it. For food, it hunted in groups, so it could probably communicate, though it is unlikely that it could talk. Unlike earlier species, it walked fully upright.

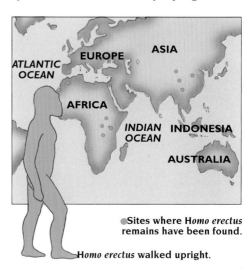

●Sites where *Homo erectus* remains have been found.

Homo erectus walked upright.

HOW DO WE KNOW?

We know about the past from the bones of people and animals which, over many thousands of years, are preserved in rock as fossils. We can also study the remains of things such as tools and buildings, which people leave behind them when they move on or die. Art, such as carvings, sculptures and cave paintings, also tells us about how people lived.

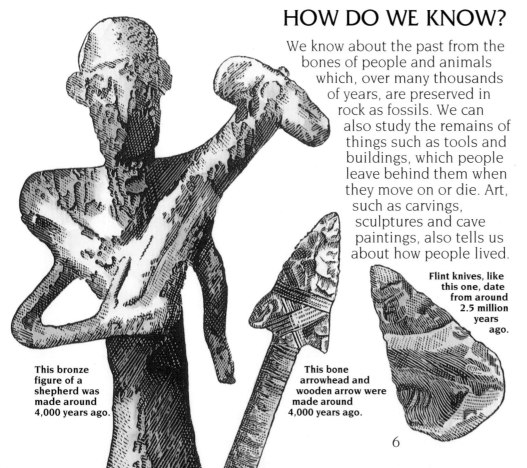

This bronze figure of a shepherd was made around 4,000 years ago.

This bone arrowhead and wooden arrow were made around 4,000 years ago.

Flint knives, like this one, date from around 2.5 million years ago.

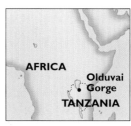

Many of the earliest human fossils have been found in the Olduvai Gorge in Tanzania, shown on the left. It was here in the 1950s that remains of *Australopithecus* were first found.

The area around the Olduvai Gorge is hot, dry grassland. In prehistoric times, it was greener and more fertile. As well as *Australopithecus*, *Homo habilis* and *Homo erectus* also lived here.

A 3.6 million year old footprint of a human ancestor, from a trail of footprints preserved in volcanic ash. It was found at Laetoli, near Olduvai Gorge, by Mary Leakey in 1978.

NEANDERTHAL MAN

By around one million years ago, a new species of human called *Homo sapiens* had developed. *Homo sapiens* means "wise man". One type of this species lived around 250,000 years ago. It is called *Homo sapiens neanderthalis*, or Neanderthal Man. Neanderthals used stone scrapers to clean animal skins for clothes and held ceremonies to bury their dead. Neanderthal people also looked after their disabled. This is known from the discovery of a man's skeleton who had lost his arm long before he died. It is unlikely that modern people developed from Neanderthal Man, but the two probably existed at the same time.

MODERN MAN

Around 200,000 years ago, *Homo sapiens sapiens*, or fully Modern Man, arrived. Scientists think that like his ancestors, he probably evolved in Africa. By around 30,000 years ago, he had spread out to every continent except Antarctica. As man's population increased, the large mammals that he hunted began to die out. People needed to find new kinds of food.

When the climate became warmer, around 10,000 years ago, people began to grow plants and breed animals for food. They no longer had to move around to find food. The age of farming had begun.

A prehistoric cave painting of a bull's head from Lascaux in France. It dates from between 20,000 and 8000BC.

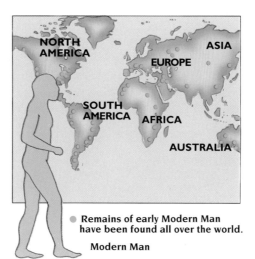
● Neanderthal remains have mainly been found in Europe.
Neanderthal Man

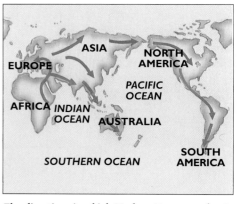
● Remains of early Modern Man have been found all over the world.
Modern Man

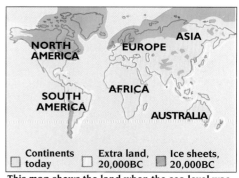
The directions in which Modern Man spread out from Africa around the world.

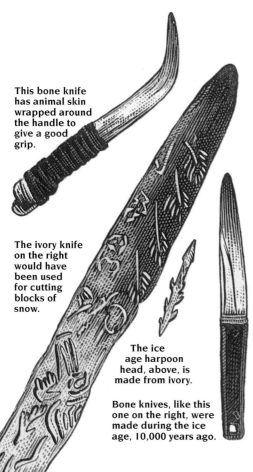
This bone knife has animal skin wrapped around the handle to give a good grip.

The ivory knife on the right would have been used for cutting blocks of snow.

The ice age harpoon head, above, is made from ivory.

Bone knives, like this one on the right, were made during the ice age, 10,000 years ago.

THE ICE AGES

In the last 3 to 4 million years, there have been nearly 20 ice ages, when the climate has been very cold and sheets of ice have covered much of the world. Ice melted and re-formed again and again. As it did so, the seas rose and fell. Environments were created and destroyed, along with many types of plants and animals. People adapted well to changes in their surroundings and that is why they survived.

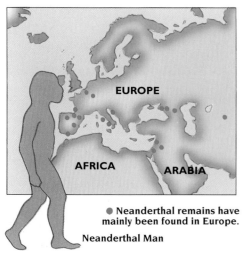
Continents today ☐ Extra land, 20,000BC ☐ Ice sheets, 20,000BC ☐
This map shows the land when the sea level was lower during the last ice age, and as it is now.

TIME CHART

4 million years ago In Africa, *Australopithecus* walks on two legs.	**250,000 years ago** Neanderthal Man evolves.	**45,000 years ago** People arrive in America.
2.5 million years ago *Homo habilis* uses tools.	**200,000 years ago** Modern Man evolves.	**35,000 years ago** Neanderthal Man dies out.
1.7 million years ago *Homo erectus* stands upright.	**100,000 years ago** Modern Man reaches Europe.	**10,000 years ago** The last ice age ends and the age of farming begins.
1 million years ago *Homo sapiens* develops.	**60,000 years ago** Man reaches Australia.	

FIND OUT MORE

Evolution   ◄ 4

Farming   ► 8

See above pages for more information.

The Standard of Ur – a monument of the Sumerians, the first civilization.

CIVILIZATION BEGINS

From 8000BC, a few small farming towns, such as Çatal Hüyük and Jericho, began to arise in Asia Minor and the Middle East. From around 3500BC, simple communities began to develop into bigger and more complex ones, and larger towns and cities arose.

A Sumerian temple, called a ziggurat.

HOW DID CIVILIZATION START?

Civilization developed at different times in different places around the world. The very first civilizations appeared in the area of Mesopotamia between the Tigris and Euphrates rivers.

The region is known as the Fertile Crescent, because the land was well watered and ideal for farming. As people began to produce more food, the population grew and people no longer had to move around in search of food.

Eventually, people learned how to use metals, especially bronze (a mixture of tin and copper), which marked the start of the Bronze Age. They also began to do specific jobs, such as building or making pots, and society became organized under leaders such as kings and priests. Trade grew between different communities and then cities became richer and grew larger.

Çatal Hüyük thrived around 6000BC. Its flat-roofed houses gave shelter to around 6,000 people.

People may have sailed up rivers and along coasts in simple boats.

In North Africa, herdsmen drove cattle. The Sahara Desert was more fertile than it is today.

| 0 | 100 | 200 | 300 | 400 | 500 | 600 km |
| 0 | | 100 | | 200 | | 300 miles |

THE SUMERIANS

The very first civilization began in Sumer, in or near the area of Mesopotamia, around 3500BC. By 3100BC, three cities had grown up – Ur, Uruk and Eridu. The Sumerians were very inventive. They were the first to use writing and they also invented the wheel.

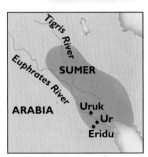

Areas of Sumerian influence around the year 2900BC.

THE BABYLONIANS

After Sumer came many empires in Mesopotamia. Around 1790BC, King Hammurabi of Babylon conquered the area, creating a Babylonian Empire. The Babylonians were excellent at many skills, including astronomy and mathematics.

The Babylonian Empire around 1792-1750BC.

THE ASSYRIANS

Around 1100BC, the Assyrians created an empire in the region. They were a cruel, aggressive people who had many enemies, including the Babylonians. After a 100 year struggle, the Assyrian Empire finally fell in 612BC, when the Babylonians destroyed its capital Nineveh.

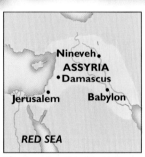

The Assyrian Empire at its greatest extent in 1076BC.

ANCIENT EGYPT

Civilization in Africa began in Egypt, along the Nile River. Around 5000BC, two farming communities developed, which gradually became organized into the Kingdoms of the Lower and Upper Nile. In 3100BC, these kingdoms were united by the pharaoh, Menes.

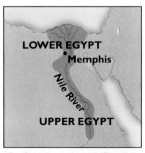

The first Egyptian civilization, around the year 3100BC.

TIME CHART

c.8000BC Farming begins in the Fertile Crescent. The small town of Jericho prospers in the Middle East.

c.7000BC People first begin to use copper in Çatal Hüyük in Asia Minor. They beat it into shaped lumps.

c.5000BC In Mesopotamia, copper and tin are mixed to make bronze for the first time.

c.3500BC The first civilization appears in Sumer.

c.3100BC Civilization appears in Egypt. The Lower and Upper Nile unite.

c.2500BC Civilization appears in the Indus Valley.

c.1800BC Civilization appears in China. In Thailand, iron is first used to make tools.

c.1790BC The Babylonians create their empire in Mesopotamia.

c.1200BC Iron is first used in the Middle East.

c.1100BC The Assyrians create their empire.

c.1000BC Iron is first used in the Mediterranean.

c.1000-600BC Civilizations begin in America.

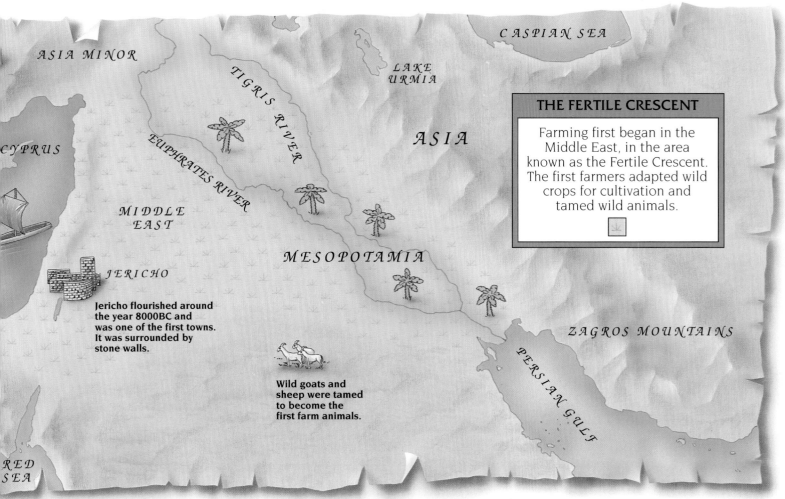

THE FERTILE CRESCENT

Farming first began in the Middle East, in the area known as the Fertile Crescent. The first farmers adapted wild crops for cultivation and tamed wild animals.

Jericho flourished around the year 8000BC and was one of the first towns. It was surrounded by stone walls.

Wild goats and sheep were tamed to become the first farm animals.

THE INDUS VALLEY

The first great Indian civilization spread along the Indus Valley, starting around 2550BC. Its leading cities were Harappa and Mohenjo-Daro. These cities had high fortresses, called citadels, inside them and large, solid houses.

The Indus Valley civilization around the year 2500BC.

SHANG CHINA

In China, civilization started around 1800BC near the Huang He River. The first civilized people were ruled by a line of kings, now called the Shang Dynasty. The people were expert workers in bronze and they traded as far away as Central Asia.

Shang Dynasty territory around 1600BC.

THE AMERICAS

The first civilizations in America began from around 1000BC. In Central America, people called the Olmecs and Zapotecs lived in large towns. In the Andes Mountains, another civilization developed around the city of Chavin. The Chavin people were expert workers in gold, silver and copper.

The Olmec, Zapotec and Chavin civilizations of America.

This gold plaque was made by the Chavin people.

ANCIENT CITIES

By 4000BC, there were flourishing farming communities throughout Europe and Asia. New materials, such as gold, copper, bronze and precious stones, were being used. People became prosperous and began to do specific jobs, such as farming or building.

A Sumerian workman making bricks from mud and straw. The bricks dried quickly in the sun.

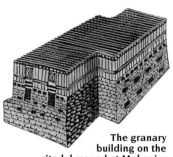

The granary building on the citadel mound at Mohenjo-Daro, where the grain was kept.

THE CITIES GROW

The success of farming and the learning of new skills meant that communities could support a bigger population. Cities became richer and trade grew between different areas.

As the wealth of these big communities grew, they became jealous of other cities. Rivalry led to warfare between different groups. To defend themselves, people built strong walls around their cities and they began to mark out their territory.

Warfare meant that the territory of some cities grew as they absorbed the territory of weaker ones. In this way, powerful cities grew into states, which became larger and larger. The first kingdoms had developed in this way and later they became the first great civilizations and empires.

UR – A SUMERIAN CITY

The city of Ur in Sumer was founded around the year 4500BC. By 2500BC it was a major trading and manufacturing city, with a population of 20,000. There was a sacred enclosure with temples and a royal palace.

Within the city walls were two artificial ports joined by canals to the Euphrates River. Unpaved streets linked the city's mud brick houses, but the streets were too narrow for wheeled vehicles.

MOHENJO-DARO

Around 2000BC, there were at least one hundred cities in northwest India. Most were fairly large, built with defensive walls of baked brick. One of the largest was Mohenjo-Daro. Like the others, it had a large central area, called a citadel, on a raised mound.

The citadel contained the religious, ceremonial and administrative buildings. It overlooked the residential area. This was divided into blocks by streets laid out in a criss-cross pattern.

THEBES – CAPITAL OF EGYPT

Thebes was the southern capital of Egypt during the New Kingdom period from 1552-1069BC. It was divided into two parts by the Nile River. The eastern half was called the City of the Living. This is where all the people lived and worked.

On the west bank of the Nile was the City of the Dead. Here were the pharaohs' temples. Nearby in the Valley of the Kings were the tombs of the pharaohs and nobles.

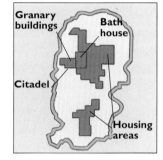

The city of Ur in Sumer. It had two man-made ports within the city walls. Trading ships used these ports.

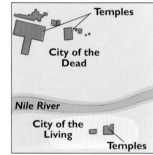

The city of Mohenjo-Daro in the Indus Valley in India. The granaries and the great bath house were on the citadel.

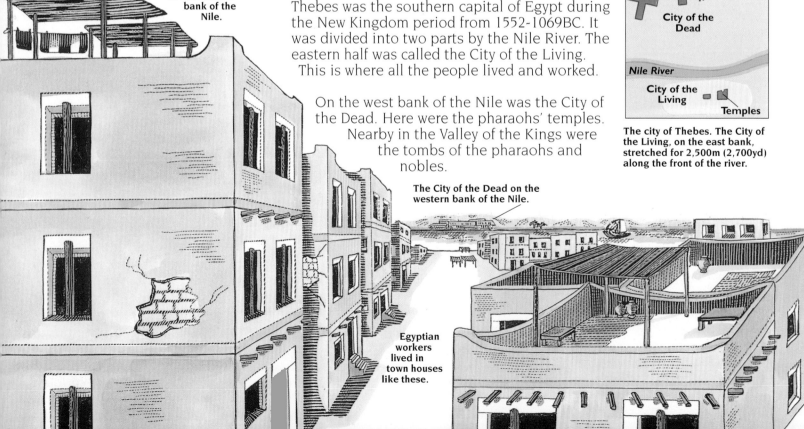

The city of Thebes. The City of the Living, on the east bank, stretched for 2,500m (2,700yd) along the front of the river.

The City of the Living on the eastern bank of the Nile.

The City of the Dead on the western bank of the Nile.

Egyptian workers lived in town houses like these.

TIME CHART

c.4500BC Ur in Sumer is founded.

c.3500BC The first civilization in the world develops in Sumer.

c.3100BC Civilization develops in Egypt.

c.2500BC Civilization appears in the Indus Valley.

c.2000BC The city of Mohenjo-Daro in the Indus Valley is abandoned.

c.1800BC The Shang Dynasty develops in China.

c.1700BC Zhengzhou, one of the six Shang capitals, is founded in China.

c.1552-1069BC Thebes is the capital of southern Egypt during the New Kingdom.

c.100BC-AD450 The city of Rome flourishes in Europe.

c.AD500 The city of Teotihuacan flourishes in Mexico. It was the sixth largest city in the world.

ZHENGZHOU IN CHINA

In northeast China, the Shang civilization developed from around 1600BC. The people kept moving their capital, so that they had six in all. One of these was called Zhengzhou. Inside its city walls were palaces and religious buildings.

The wall was made of packed earth, 7km (4 miles) long and over 9m (30ft) high. Outside were the residential areas and work areas, with specialist shops where people made bone, pottery and bronze objects.

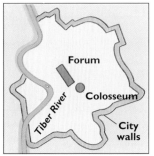

The city of Zhengzhou, one of the six Shang capitals. The residential area was outside the walled city enclosure.

ROME – THE LARGEST CITY

Rome, the capital of the huge Roman Empire, was the largest city in the ancient world. It had a population of over one million people between the 1st and the 4th centuries AD.

Rome had over 44,000 apartment buildings, 1,000 bath houses and ten aqueducts (bridges to carry water). The city's boundaries were marked by city walls and a short stretch of the Tiber River. Altogether they measured 17km (10 miles).

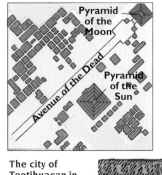

Rome in Italy. The Colosseum and the Forum were two of the most important buildings in the city.

TEOTIHUACAN

In AD500, Teotihuacan in Mexico was the sixth largest city in the world. It had a population of 200,000 and was the capital of a Mexican empire which controlled central Mexico. It covered 20 square km (8 square miles). A wide avenue ran from north to south, called the Avenue of the Dead, which was over 5km (3 miles) long. It was lined with over 75 pyramids, which were topped with temples.

In the middle of the city there was a huge ceremonial, military and administrative area. The palaces of the rulers were also in the same area.

The city of Teotihuacan in Mexico. It was laid out in a grid pattern.

The largest pyramid in Teotihuacan is called the Pyramid of the Sun. It was 70m (230 feet) high.

The pyramids were made from soil and rubble and then covered with stone. They were then painted red and white. The Pyramid of the Sun contained over 1,000,000 m³ (35,000,000 cubic ft) of material.

TRADE ROUTES

As manufacturing grew, trade between distant communities developed. By AD500, there were well established communication routes throughout Europe and Asia.

The Indus Valley and Mesopotamia in the Middle East traded together, transporting goods by sea. Seals have been found in the Indus Valley from Mesopotamia, and vice versa, which prove this. There were also well-defined trade routes for bullock carts stretching overland from the Indus Valley to Afghanistan and Persia.

A clay pot, made in Sumer in Mesopotamia around 2500BC.

In South America, at the period when Teotihuacan flourished, there were trading posts throughout Mexico. These trading posts link cities in Mexico to the Pacific coast.

There were temples on top of the pyramids, where people went to worship their gods.

Smaller pyramids lining the Avenue of the Dead.

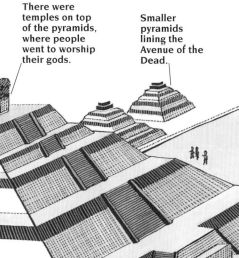

LANGUAGES

Today, there are over 10,000 different languages. Over the centuries, many have died out and many more have developed. We know about some early languages from writing, which began 6,000 years ago.

Sumerian writing from about 2800BC, detailing lists of fields and crops.

Linear writing, found on the island of Crete about 2000BC.

LANGUAGE FAMILIES

Languages can be grouped into families. All the languages in one particular family will have developed from the same language in the past. For example, French and Spanish both developed from Latin around 1500 years ago. The maps on this page show the largest families and some of the languages which belong to them. In America and Australia there were originally thousands of native languages, but most have died out. In these areas English, Spanish or Portuguese are the main languages, taken there by European settlers.

Experts think that language developed hundreds of thousands of years ago. As people migrated or invaded different areas, their language will have moved with them. Language changes very quickly, so as different groups came into contact with each other, their languages will have evolved. For example, it is known that as people from the Steppes grasslands region migrated across Europe, their words associated with their knowledge of horses spread across Europe with them.

The Hamito-Semitic group. Ancient Egyptian belonged to this group.

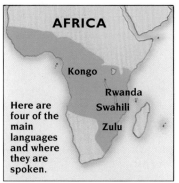
The Niger-Congo group. There are thousands of languages in this group.

The Indo-European languages were taken far and wide by Europeans.

The Uralian group. This group originated in Russia, on the borders of Europe and Asia.

The Malayo-Polynesian group. This covers a vast area of the Pacific.

The Turkic-Mongolian-Tungus group. This has 40 or so languages.

The Dravidian group. This group has over 20 languages.

The Steppes grasslands in central Asia. Nomads from here migrated west thousands of years ago. Their language spread into Europe.

INDO-EUROPEAN LANGUAGES

One of the major families is called the Indo-European group. It includes some Asian languages and many European ones. Experts think that it originated in Mesopotamia and spread out into Europe and India. When the Huns and other nomad invaders came to Europe in the 5th century AD, they brought their languages with them from northeast Asia. This divided the Indo-European group into east and west. However, there are still similarities between all the languages in this group.

A Hun horseman. Huns were nomads who migrated west from Asia in the 4th and 5th centuries AD.

The Sino-Tibetan group. It includes Chinese – one of the most spoken languages.

WRITING BEGINS

The ability to write is one of the skills that helped early civilizations to develop. The first written symbols were used in Sumer between 4000 and 3000BC. They were simple pictures of objects, called pictograms. Writing was first used to record the possessions of kings, but it was also soon used to record events.

THE FIRST WRITING

Each early civilization developed its own system of writing, based on different characters.

EUROPE

Linear writing from Crete

Sumerian pictograms

CRETE

EGYPT

SUMER

ARABIA

AFRICA

HIMALAYAS

Indus Valley glyphs

Ancient Chinese symbols

CHINA

INDIA

Indian Ocean

Egyptian hieroglyphics

N
W   E
S

0   1000   2000   3000 km

0   500   1000   1500 miles

Sumerian writing, on a block of clay, called a tablet. Sumerian pictograms were drawn with a sharpened reed.

SUMER

As time went by, pictograms were replaced by symbols which stood for objects but did not look like them. In Sumer these symbols were drawn on clay. This wedge-shaped writing is called cuneiform, after the Latin word *cuneus*, meaning wedge. It was also used in Assyria and Babylonia.

EGYPT

In Ancient Egypt, pictograms were first used to represent objects and later used to stand for sounds. Egyptian symbols are called hieroglyphics, which means "sacred carvings". Priests controlled what was written, and writing was mainly used for inscriptions on tombs and monuments.

CHINA

In China, writing also developed from simple pictograms, which were used for objects and sounds. In China today, there are thousands of characters, called ideograms, in daily use. Ideograms are symbols which stand for an idea or a thing. Writing in Korea and Japan also developed in this way.

THE ROMAN ALPHABET

Around 2000BC, a script with only 27 characters was invented in Canaan in the Middle East. It was an alphabetic script, where each symbol stood for a single consonant. This system was adopted by the Greeks, who added vowel signs. Later on, the Romans adapted it and it is now known as the Roman alphabet.

Wedge-shaped cuneiform symbols from Sumer.

An Egyptian hieroglyphic symbol. It stood for a sound.

The Chinese symbol for "tree", based on the shape of branches.

A Russian cyrillic character – a variation of the Roman alphabet.

TIME CHART

c.6000-5000BC Indo-Europeans spread out from Asia Minor into Europe.

c.4000-1000BC Indo-Europeans spread out into Asia and deeper into Europe.

c.4000BC Pictograms are first used in Sumer.

c.3200BC Writing begins in Egypt.

c.3000BC Cuneiform writing is used in Sumer, Assyria and Babylonia.

c.2000BC Alphabetic script is invented in Canaan, in the Middle East.

c.2000BC Pictograms are used in India.

c.2000-1400BC Two forms of picture writing, called Linear A and Linear B, are used on the Mediterranean island of Crete.

c.1500BC Pictograms are used in China.

c.1100BC Phoenicians develop an alphabet.

c.700BC Alphabetic script is adapted by the Romans.

c.500BC Cuneiform writing begins to die out.

c.AD300-500 Huns and other Asian nomads invade Europe. Indo-European languages begin to divide into two groups – east and west.

FIND OUT MORE

Egypt	▶ 14
Romans	▶ 18
Shang China	◀ 9
Sumer	◀ 8

See above pages for more information.

ANCIENT EGYPT

The Ancient Egyptian civilization spanned nearly 3,000 years, from 3300BC to 332BC. Egyptian society was highly organized and life was mostly based on farming settlements around the Nile River. The Egyptians also built towns and cities with elaborate monuments.

An early Egyptian reed boat.

Queen Nefertiti, wife of Pharaoh Akhenaten who reigned between 1364 and 1347BC.

THE OLD KINGDOM

Egyptian history is divided into periods, depending on which families of pharaohs (kings) ruled Egypt. Over the centuries, times of stable government, called Kingdoms, were followed by times of trouble and insecurity. These troubled times are known as the Intermediate Periods.

One of the greatest periods of Egyptian history was the Old Kingdom. This period lasted from around 2649BC until 2150BC. The pyramids (burial monuments of the pharaohs) were built during this time and the empire was run by a strong central government. Egypt was divided into 42 areas called *nomes*, which were ruled by powerful officials. The officials kept their positions for life and passed them on to their sons when they died. This meant that they enjoyed a strong position in Egyptian society.

The officials became more and more powerful, and eventually they challenged the authority of the pharaohs. The government collapsed and this breakdown led to the First Intermediate Period.

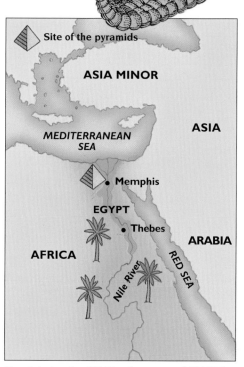

Egypt during the Old Kingdom, around 2200BC. At this time the capital was Memphis.

THE EMPIRE GROWS

During the First Intermediate Period, Egypt was invaded and there were bitter disputes over who should rule it. Around 2040BC the government became stronger and the capital was moved to Thebes. This was the start of the Middle Kingdom, when Egypt occupied Nubia. Egypt then grew to its greatest extent under Tuthmosis III (c.1490-1436BC) in the New Kingdom.

In 664BC, Egypt entered a new era of peace and prosperity in the Late Period. Trade was successful and foreigners were encouraged to settle in Egypt. Then in 525BC, the pharaoh was defeated by the Emperor of Persia. The Ancient Egyptian age finally ended when Alexander the Great of Macedon conquered Egypt. He made it successful once more and Egypt continued to be ruled by Macedonian pharaohs until it fell to the Roman Empire in 30BC.

Tutenkhamun reigned from 1347-1337BC. His tomb was famously discovered in the 1920s.

A coin showing the conqueror Alexander the Great, who reigned from 336-323BC.

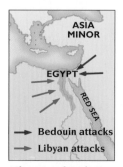

Libyans and Bedouins invaded in the First Intermediate Period.

Egypt and Nubia during the Middle Kingdom.

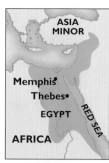

Egypt's greatest extent during Tuthmosis III's New Kingdom.

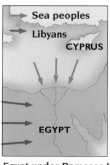

Egypt under Rameses II (1289-1224BC) was weakened by invasions.

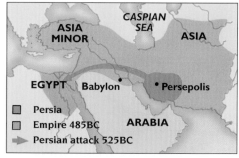

The Persian invasion in 525BC. The Persians ruled Egypt until 404BC, and then again from 341-332BC.

Ma'at – goddess of justice and truth. She represented harmony and balance in the Universe.

TEMPLES

The Egyptians built huge temples as homes for their many gods. Only priests and priestesses were allowed to go inside the temples. Ordinary people went to the temple entrances to pray and bring offerings for the gods.

Many gods were identified with animals and are often shown with animal heads in wall paintings. Each god's animal was kept in his or her temple and was treated with great respect by the people.

FARMING

Farming was entirely dependent on the Nile River to provide water and make the land fertile. Every spring, the Nile became swollen with rain water. By July, the river flooded, spreading water and rich soil over the fields, which helped the next year's crops to grow.

After the floods had gone, seeds were sown. Crops were watered through long ditches, called irrigation channels, which brought water from the Nile.

TRAVEL

Most Egyptians lived within easy reach of the Nile, so they used boats and ships to travel from place to place. The boats and ships were built from reeds and wood.

To go north, the Egyptians allowed their boats to drift downstream toward the sea. The wind blew from north to south, so when they wanted to go south, they used sails to move against the current. Ships were steered with a large oar at the stern.

Amun was the King of the Gods in the New Kingdom.

Irrigation channels brought water from the Nile to the fields.

A New Kingdom trading ship.

THE PYRAMIDS

Egyptians believed in life after death and that to survive in the next world, the body had to stay intact. To achieve this pharaohs and rich noblemen built huge stone pyramids to house their bodies and possessions when they died. Bodies were preserved by embalming them (soaking them in oil) and wrapping them in cloth. These bodies, called mummies, were then placed in decorated coffins and entombed inside the pyramid. The Great Pyramid of King Cheops was built from over two million stones.

Pyramids, though, were often robbed by treasure-hunters. So pharaohs in the later New Kingdom were buried in tombs cut secretly into the sides of cliffs. Tutenkhamun's tomb was one of these.

See above pages for more information.

Pyramids were built from stone and originally covered in white limestone.

The dead king was buried in a tomb. After burial, the passages were sealed.

False tombs might have been built to confuse grave robbers.

THE ANCIENT GREEKS

The first Greek civilizations were those of the Minoans and Mycenaeans. The Minoans lived in Crete and the Mycenaeans in mainland Greece. Successful both in warfare and trade, the early Greek kings built rich palaces. Nearby were farms and craftsmen's workshops.

A Greek soldier, called a hoplite, from the 6th century BC.

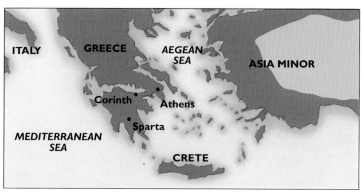

The Parthenon – the temple on the Acropolis in Athens, built around 440BC. It was dedicated to the goddess Athene and had a huge statue of her inside.

THE GREEK CITY-STATES

Around 1100BC, some Greeks migrated from mainland Greece to islands in the Aegean Sea and to the coast of Asia Minor. For 300 years civilization declined and many skills were lost. The Greeks were no longer ruled by kings, but by small groups of nobles called oligarchies, which ruled their own regions.

From 800BC conditions improved. Coins were minted and writing was rediscovered. Communities became small states called city-states, which had their own laws, armies, money and local gods, but shared the same language and religion. Also, colonists were sent out to found new cities.

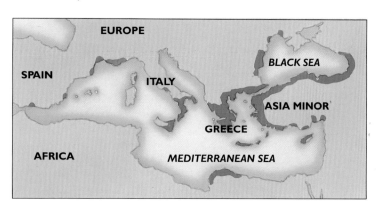

By 550BC, the Greeks had colonized new cities around the edge of the Mediterranean.

The three most powerful city-states were Corinth, Sparta and Athens. A city-state consisted of the city and its surrounding countryside.

THE PERSIAN WARS

A Persian archer from the 6th century BC.

Around this time, the new power of Persia was growing in Asia. The empire included the Greek cities of Asia Minor, called the Ionian cities. In 498BC, Athens helped the Ionian cities in an attempt to break free from Persia. They were soon defeated, but the Persian Emperor Darius was determined to punish Athens. In 490BC he sent a fleet of ships to do battle. His forces landed at Marathon, where the Athenians won a surprise victory. When Darius died, his son Xerxes sent an even bigger fleet and a huge army against Athens. The city was destroyed, but Persia was beaten at Salamis in 480BC and at Plataea in 479BC. The Ionian cities were then able to regain their freedom.

An oar-powered boat called a trireme. The Greeks and the Persians fought in these.

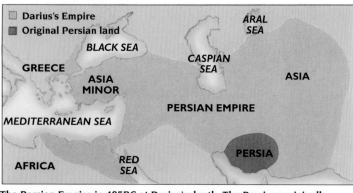

The Persian Empire in 485BC at Darius's death. The Persians originally came from the area which is now part of modern day Iran.

The Persian invasion routes and the major battle sites between the Greeks and the Persians. The wars lasted from 490-449BC.

THE DELIAN LEAGUE

The Persians continued to threaten the Greeks, so Athens organized a union against them in 478BC. It was made up of the Ionian cities and the Aegean islands, known together as the Delian League. Over the years, it developed into an Athenian Empire. In 449BC Persia and Athens agreed peace.

From 508BC a new system of government, called democracy, developed in Athens. Free male citizens were given a right to vote. Slaves, however, were used more and more frequently in trade and farming.

The Delian League, named after Delos, where its treasury was.

ATHENS AGAINST SPARTA

Sparta was also powerful and had its own allies, known as the Peloponnesian League. In 431BC, war broke out between Athens and Sparta. Sparta was eventually the victor, but only after abandoning the Ionian cities to Persia. They did this in return for enough funds from Persia to finish the war against Athens.

Sparta's attempts to be the leading city in all Greece failed. Its arrogance and brutality quickly turned the other cities against it. Athens then began to recover some of its former power.

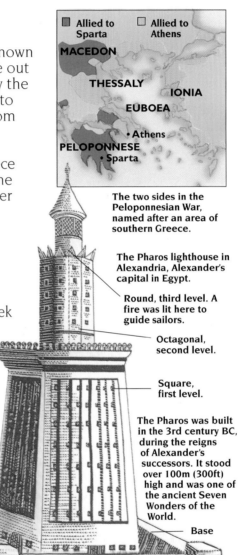

The two sides in the Peloponnesian War, named after an area of southern Greece.

The Pharos lighthouse in Alexandria, Alexander's capital in Egypt.

Round, third level. A fire was lit here to guide sailors.

Octagonal, second level.

Square, first level.

The Pharos was built in the 3rd century BC, during the reigns of Alexander's successors. It stood over 100m (300ft) high and was one of the ancient Seven Wonders of the World.

Base

ALEXANDER THE GREAT

A new power soon arose in Greece – Macedon, an almost barbaric state in the north of Greece. Its cunning king, Philip, realized that the feuding Greek cities would be no match for his army. He soon became the supreme power. Philip was later assassinated, but his son Alexander took over. He made sure that Greece would not rebel against him by razing the city of Thebes to the ground. After this, no other city challenged him.

In 334BC, Alexander set out for Persia. He shattered the forces of Darius III and for the next eleven years, he marched through Africa and Asia, founding many cities, some of which were called Alexandria. Scientists and surveyors went with him, learning about geography, plants and animals. When Alexander died in Babylon in 323BC his empire was divided. Areas of it later became part of the Roman Empire.

TIME CHART

c.1450BC Peak of the first Greek civilization.

c.1100BC Dorian people from the northwest invade southern Greece and Crete, causing many mainland Greeks to migrate

1100-800BC The Dark Age, when Greek culture declined.

c.850BC The Greeks begin to colonize Asia Minor and set up cities around the Mediterranean coast.

c.850-750BC The poet Homer tells the traditional story about the Trojan War (c.1100BC).

522-485BC Reign of the Persian King Darius I.

498-449BC Persia is at war with Athens.

c.460BC Democracy is established in Athens.

431-404BC Athens fights against Sparta in the Peloponnesian War.

371-362BC Thebes becomes the dominant power in Greece.

359-336BC Reign of Philip of Macedon.

336BC Philip is assassinated.

336-323BC Reign of Alexander the Great.

334BC Alexander sets out to conquer his empire.

333BC Alexander defeats Persian King Darius III.

330BC Death of King Darius III.

327BC Alexander reaches India.

323BC Alexander dies in Babylon.

323-281BC Alexander's successors fight over territory.

281BC Three kingdoms emerge from Alexander's former empire – the Kingdoms of Ptolemy, Antigonas and Seleucus.

147-146BC Macedon and Greece become Roman provinces.

Macedon, the area in northern Greece from which Philip originated.

Philip of Macedon's Empire in 336BC at the time of his assassination.

The extent of Alexander the Great's Empire at his death in 323BC.

FIND OUT MORE

Greek religion	▶ 22
Roman Empire	▶ 18

See above pages for more information.

THE ROMAN EMPIRE

Hannibal the Carthaginian used elephants in his army against the Roman Empire.

In Latium, the central plain on Italy's west coast, a group of villages grew up near an island in the Tiber River. It was a convenient place to cross the Tiber and it was here that Rome was built. According to legend, it was founded in 753BC by Romulus after he killed his twin brother Remus. Romulus became Rome's first king.

A glass vessel, from the 3rd century AD, made by Roman craftsmen.

THE REPUBLIC

Rome was governed by kings until 510BC, when the people banished them. It then became a republic, governed by a group of citizens, called the Senate. Rome was the dominant city in Latium, defended by a city wall and a strong army.

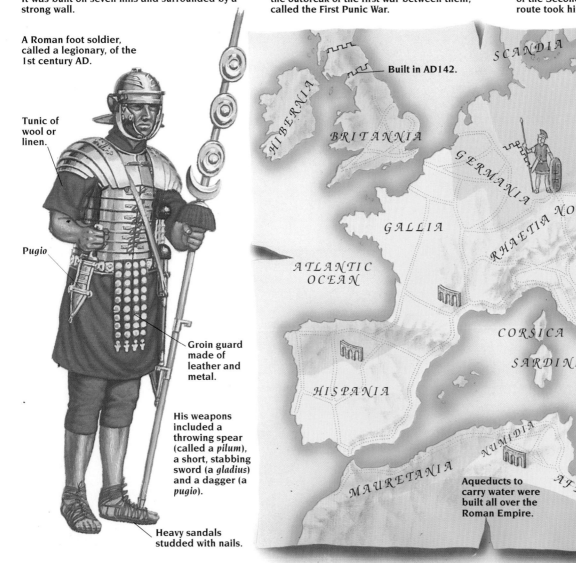

By 338BC, Rome was the leading city in Latium. It was built on seven hills and surrounded by a strong wall.

ROME EXPANDS

By 272BC, Rome controlled all of Italy. War then broke out with the powerful Carthaginian Empire. The Romans pushed Carthage out of Sicily, Sardinia and Corsica, but Carthage managed to gain some territory in Spain.

Roman and Carthaginian territory in 264BC, at the outbreak of the first war between them, called the First Punic War.

To attack Rome, a Carthaginian general called Hannibal led an army and a troop of elephants from Spain across the Alps to Italy. There he won many battles against the Roman army, but was never able to attack Rome itself.

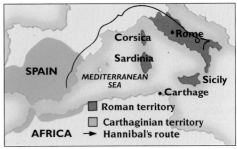

The Roman and Carthaginian Empires at the start of the Second Punic War in 218BC. Hannibal's route took him all the way across the Alps.

A Roman foot soldier, called a legionary, of the 1st century AD.

Tunic of wool or linen.

Pugio

Groin guard made of leather and metal.

His weapons included a throwing spear (called a *pilum*), a short, stabbing sword (a *gladius*) and a dagger (a *pugio*).

Heavy sandals studded with nails.

Built in AD142.

"Barbarian" tribes in central Europe raided the empire's borders.

Aqueducts to carry water were built all over the Roman Empire.

TIME CHART

800BC Etruscans from Asia Minor settle in Italy.	**272BC** Tarentum surrenders and Rome controls Italy.	**202BC** Carthage is captured.	**AD98-117** Trajan is emperor.
753BC The city of Rome is founded.	**241BC** Rome occupies Sicily, Corsica and Sardinia.	**60BC** The First Triumvirate rules.	**AD117-138** Hadrian is emperor.
510BC Kings are banished from Rome by the people.	**218BC** Hannibal crosses the Alps.	**44BC** Julius Caesar is murdered on March 15 – the Ides of March.	**AD138-161** Antoninus Pius is emperor. Rome's power is at its peak.
282BC War breaks out between Rome and Tarentum.	**206BC** Rome captures Spain.	**31BC-AD14** Augustus, the first Roman Emperor, rules.	**AD193** Throne auctioned to Didius Julianus, who is later murdered.

UNREST IN ROME

By 100BC, the Roman Empire included Spain, southern Gaul, Greece, Africa (modern Tunisia) and Asia Minor. The Senate, though, found the huge empire hard to run and there was unrest at home in Italy.

Back home, soldiers found their farms ruined. They had to take their families to find work in Rome where crime and unemployment were high. People were unhappy and soldiers were loyal to their generals, not the Senate.

JULIUS CAESAR

In 60BC, a group of three men took control. One of them was Julius Caesar – a great soldier. In 49BC, civil war erupted and Caesar gained power. The Senate voted him ruler for life, but soon after, he was stabbed to death by rivals.

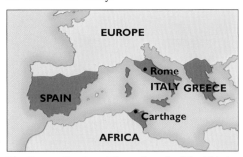

The Roman Empire at the outbreak of the Third Punic War in 149BC. Only Carthage was left of the Carthaginian Empire and Rome destroyed it.

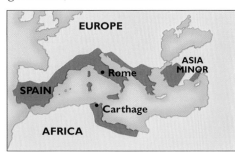

The Roman Empire in 80BC. By this time the Romans had begun to acquire territory in Asia Minor.

Caesar was best known for the conquest of Gaul (modern day France) between 58 and 50BC. He also invaded Britain in both 55 and 54BC.

THE EMPIRE AT ITS PEAK

In 31BC, Caesar's heir, Octavian became the first Roman Emperor, taking the name Augustus in 27BC. He set up a military dictatorship that was to last for the next 500 years. The Romans made more conquests until the empire reached its largest extent in AD117, during the rule of Emperor Trajan.

For some time, Rome was peaceful and wealthy, although many citizens were poor and miserable. Also, tribes in central Europe were jealous of the empire and raided its borders. Rome had to raise taxes to pay for soldiers to defend it. The mighty Roman Empire then fell into a long, gradual decline.

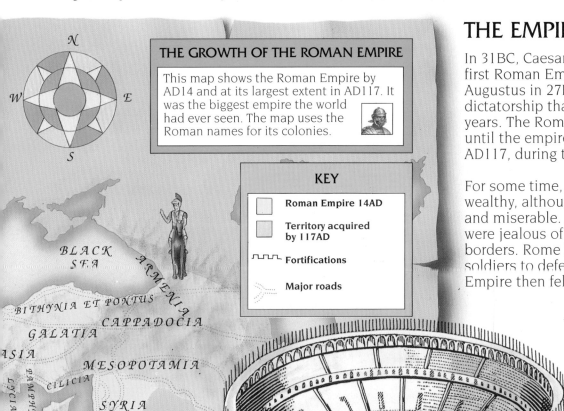

THE GROWTH OF THE ROMAN EMPIRE

This map shows the Roman Empire by AD14 and at its largest extent in AD117. It was the biggest empire the world had ever seen. The map uses the Roman names for its colonies.

KEY

- Roman Empire 14AD
- Territory acquired by 117AD
- Fortifications
- Major roads

BLACK SEA
ARMENIA
BITHYNIA ET PONTUS
CAPPADOCIA
GALATIA
ASIA
MESOPOTAMIA
LYCIA
PAMPHYLIA
CILICIA
CYPRUS
SYRIA
AEGYPTUS
ARABIA

The Colosseum in Rome. This building was used to stage fights and games for the Roman public to watch.

THE GREAT INVADERS

From the 3rd century AD, nomadic tribes from central Europe began to attack the frontiers of the Roman Empire. The Romans called these uncivilized invaders "barbarians". As well as barbarian attacks, civil wars, taxation, famine and disease all weakened the empire.

Barbarian invaders used spears, and bows and arrows like these.

This clasp for clothing was made by barbarians around 500AD.

THE EMPIRE DIVIDES

To safeguard the frontiers of the Roman Empire from barbarian invasions, Emperor Diocletian decided to make the army bigger. He also decided to split the empire in two to make it easier to rule. Diocletian ruled the eastern half, while his fellow soldier, Maximian, ruled the west. Each ruler, called an Augustus, had a deputy called a Caesar.

In AD305, Diocletian abdicated. Four rival leaders emerged, one of whom was called Constantine. He marched from where he was stationed in Britain to claim a share of the empire. Constantine believed that dividing the empire was wrong. He set about becoming the sole ruler and uniting east and west by fighting his rivals. He became sole Emperor in AD323.

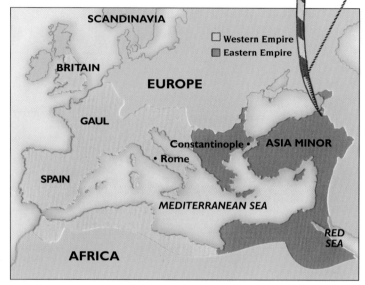

The division of the Roman Empire around AD293. It was now split into east and west.

CONSTANTINE'S REIGN

During his fight to become the sole ruler of the empire, Constantine is said to have seen a vision of a cross. This happened before the Battle of Milvian Bridge in AD312, which he went on to win. Constantine believed that the vision was a sign from Christ and from then on he encouraged Christianity in the empire. However, he was not baptized a Christian until shortly before his death.

While waging his wars, Constantine used up much of the wealth of the west. So he founded a new capital in the still rich east, at Byzantium. He renamed the city Constantinople after himself. After his death though, the empire divided again.

Iron and copper helmet

Gothic invaders from the 4th century AD.

Gothic fighters wore iron chainmail vests, called corselets.

THE BARBARIANS INVADE

Far away in central Asia, a fearless, tough tribe of nomads called the Huns began to conquer new land. As they did so, they drove before them other Asian tribes. These barbarian tribes spread in all directions. They invaded China, Persia and India, causing great damage to the civilizations there.

In AD367, the barbarians poured across the Rhine and the Danube into the Roman Empire. Many set up their own kingdoms as Rome's power crumbled. Unable to get rid of them, Emperor Theodosius made peace. He offered to make them part of the empire, as long as they provided workers and soldiers.

THE NEW KINGDOMS

In AD451, the Roman general Aetius won the last great Roman victory when he defeated Attila the Hun at Châlons in central France. In AD455, Rome was sacked by Vandal pirates and by AD476, the western empire was finished. The last emperor of the west was deposed and Europe was now a much changed place. In place of the Roman Empire were lots of smaller kingdoms, ruled by the barbarians.

Britain was now in the hands of the Jutes, Angles and Saxons who had invaded from Denmark and Germany. France was occupied by the Burgundians and the Franks, who were also from Germany. Spain had been overrun by the Vandals, who then settled in north Africa. Spain itself was later ruled by the Visigoths. A related tribe, called the Ostrogoths, occupied southeast Europe and Italy.

Route
Settlement area

The Jutes, Angles and Saxons invaded Britain from Denmark and north Germany.

The Franks invaded Gaul (modern day France) from their home in Germany.

The Vandals rode from Asia into Europe. They eventually settled in Africa.

The Goths came from Asia. The western Goths, or Visigoths, settled in Spain.

The eastern Goths, or Ostrogoths, invaded southeastern Europe and settled in Italy.

THE BYZANTINE EMPIRE

The eastern half of the Roman Empire survived to become a new power – the Byzantine Empire. Like the old empire, it had a strong military system, an orderly government and it followed Christianity. Gradually, it gained its own identity. Greek became its official language and its eastern Orthodox Church developed from the western Roman Catholic one. The literature of Ancient Greece and Rome was preserved in its libraries, and art and learning also flourished.

In AD527, an emperor called Justinian came to the Byzantine throne. He then set out to conquer the old western Roman provinces. He recaptured much of the old territories, but his victories cost the Byzantine Empire much wealth. After Justinian died in AD565, his reconquests were lost again within a century.

A 6th century mosaic from the Church of San Vitale in Ravenna, Italy, showing Emperor Justinian.

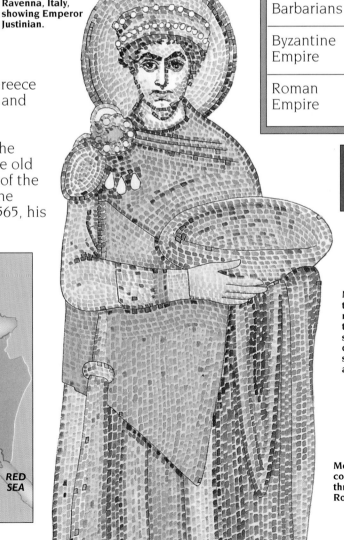

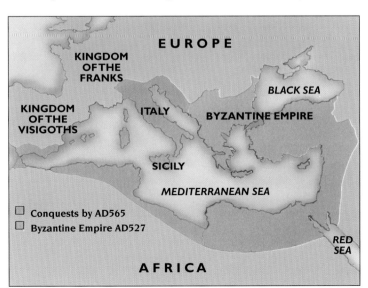

Justinian's Byzantine Empire on his succession in AD527 and at his death in AD565. He reconquered part of the old Roman Empire.

TIME CHART

AD200 Barbarians begin to attack Britain.

AD293 Diocletian divides empire into eastern and western halves.

AD300 Romans begin to build forts on coasts of southern England and northern France to keep out invaders.

AD306-37 Reign of Emperor Constantine, who reunites the empire.

AD330 Constantinople becomes new capital of the Roman Empire.

AD367 Barbarians cross Rhine and Danube.

AD391 Christianity becomes the official religion of the Roman Empire.

AD451 General Aetius defeats Attila the Hun.

AD527-65 Reign of Byzantine Emperor Justinian.

AD535-55 Justinian captures North Africa, Italy and Spain.

FIND OUT MORE

Barbarians	▶ 26
Byzantine Empire	▶ 30
Roman Empire	◀ 18

See above pages for more information.

Mosaics like this were made from tiny pieces of stone of different shades, set in a cement.

Mosaics were common throughout the Roman world.

WORLD RELIGIONS

All civilizations developed their own religions. Religions helped people to explain questions about how the world was created, birth and death, good and evil and why life is like it is.

Figure of an ancient goddess. This stone carving is 25,000 years old.

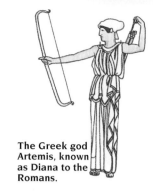
The Greek god Artemis, known as Diana to the Romans.

ANCIENT GODS

Many ancient religions have now died out. Some were based upon the worship of many gods and goddesses. The Sumerians had hundreds of gods, who had to be obeyed and given gifts or sacrifices. The Egyptians believed that over 2,000 gods and goddesses governed every part of human life.

The Sumerian and Egyptian Empires around 3000BC.

GREEKS AND ROMANS

Most ancient religions did not spread far. Greek and Roman religion, however, spread over the Greek world and the Roman Empire. Greek gods were associated with life and nature. The Romans then merged them with their own so that many have two names, a Greek one and a Roman one.

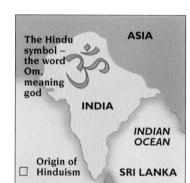
The Roman Empire, around the year 27BC.

INDIA, CHINA AND JAPAN

Hinduism, one of the world's great religions, began in India, around 2500BC. Its followers worship many gods, who are all believed to be different forms of one great being, called "Brahman". Hinduism's most important gods are Brahma the Creator, Vishnu the Preserver and Siva the Destroyer.

A second world religion, Buddhism, also began in India. Buddhism is based on the teachings of a man called Siddhartha Gautama, or the Buddha ("the enlightened one"), who lived in India in the 6th century BC. It later spread from India into China and Southeast Asia.

Today, Buddhism is still strong in China and Southeast Asia, though it has nearly disappeared in India. It is the only major world religion which does not focus on a god or several gods, but on the teachings of a philosopher (great thinker). In China, two other religions are also based on the teachings of great philosophers. These religions are Taoism and Confucianism.

In Japan, an ancient religion called Shintoism dates from before the 7th century BC. It was based on a desire to be at one with nature and it demanded obedience to the emperor, who was believed to be a descendant of the sun goddess. Other important ideas in the Shinto religion are the worship of traditional Japanese heroes and people's family ancestors.

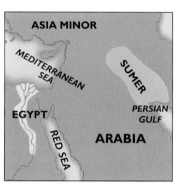
Krishna, a form of the Hindu god Brahman.

Krishna is the most celebrated of the Hindu gods.

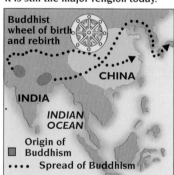
Hinduism originated in India, where it is still the major religion today.

Buddhism began in India and spread into China.

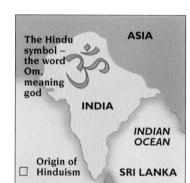
Shintoism, which is based solely in Japan, did not spread elsewhere.

JUDAISM

Traditionally, Judaism is the religion of the Jews – first known as the Israelites, who established themselves in 1274BC in Canaan in the Middle East. They conquered Canaan about 1000BC and

A candlestick, called a menorah, used in Jewish religious ceremonies.

made it their homeland, with Jerusalem as their capital. The north of Canaan became known as Israel, while the south was called Judah.

After defeat by the Babylonians in 586BC, the Israelites began to spread out over Europe and the Mediterranean. They continued to spread out during the time of the Roman Empire. The Israelites became known as the Jews and this movement of people is called the Diaspora. Although they were away from home, the Jews kept their religion, based on their belief of their special relationship with the one, true God.

The Jewish holy scriptures, the Torah and the Talmud, are written on scrolls.

CHRISTIANITY

In the Middle East, around AD30, a new religion called Christianity developed. A group of men called the apostles began to spread the teachings of a Jew called Jesus Christ. They preached that Christ had risen from the dead following his execution by the Romans. They proclaimed Christ to be the Son of God who had died to save his people. Their message spread quickly.

Jesus Christ, founder of Christianity.

During the time of the Roman Empire, there were periods when Christianity was banned. This was because the Romans wanted everyone to worship the emperor as a god. The Christians refused, believing that they should not worship any other god but theirs.

Christians were often killed or persecuted. Christianity, though, was later tolerated and then became the official religion of the Roman Empire in AD391.

THE BIRTH OF ISLAM

In Mecca in Arabia in AD570, a man called Muhammad was born. He preached that his fellow Arabs should stop the worship of idols (false gods) and submit to the will of God, or Allah. During his lifetime, Muhammad claimed that he received messages from Allah, which he wrote down word for word.

Allah's words, known as the Ko'ran, became the guiding principles of a new religion – Islam. By Muhammad's death in AD632, Islam influenced most of Arabia. It later spread to Africa and Asia.

A tile from a mosque in Istanbul, decorated with verses from the Ko'ran.

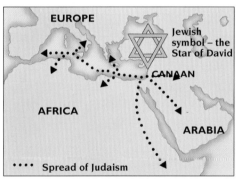

Over the centuries, the Jewish people spread out in all directions from their homeland in Canaan.

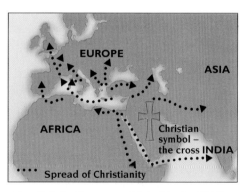

After Christianity was established in the Middle East it spread mainly into Africa and Europe.

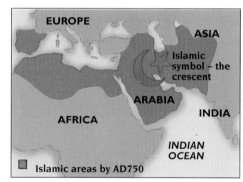

Islam originated in Arabia and by AD750, it had spread into Asia, north Africa and Spain.

TIME CHART

2500BC Hinduism begins in India.

2000BC According to Jewish tradition, God speaks to Abraham, the father of Judaism.

1274BC Jews settle in Canaan.

c.604-531BC Life of Lao-Tse, founder of Taoism.

600BC By this time, Shintoism has been established.

586BC The Jewish Diaspora begins.

550-480BC Life of Siddhartha Gautama – the Buddha.

551-479BC Life of Confucius – founder of Confucianism.

c.0-AD30 Life of Jesus Christ, founder of Christianity.

AD391 Emperor Theodosius makes Christianity the official religion of the Roman Empire.

AD570-632 Life of Muhammad, founder of Islam.

AD622 Muhammad and his followers arrive in Medina after being forced out of Mecca. This date marks the start of the Islamic religion.

AD750 Islam has spread throughout Arabia and north Africa. It also spread into Asia and into Spain.

FIND OUT MORE

See above pages for more information.

GREAT EMPIRES

As Europe recovered from the fall of Rome, great empires flourished in Asia, America and Africa. In Asia, the T'ang Dynasty was a golden age for Chinese culture. In America, the Maya were building great monuments, while in Africa, great trading empires developed.

The Chinese explored in ships like this one, called junks.

T'ANG CHINA

In AD618, China was united under an imperial family called the T'ang Dynasty. The T'ang era became one of the greatest periods of Chinese history. It was a time of inventions, such as printing, porcelain, the magnetic compass, paper money and gunpowder.

Then in 907, the T'ang Dynasty fell to invaders and a troubled period followed. China was later reunited under the Sung Dynasty, until nomads in the north set up the Ch'in Empire. China eventually fell to the Mongols by the end of the 13th century.

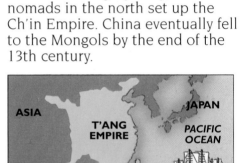

ASIA
JAPAN
T'ANG EMPIRE
PACIFIC OCEAN
INDIA

The T'ang Empire in China in the 8th century. From here, the Chinese set out to explore Asia.

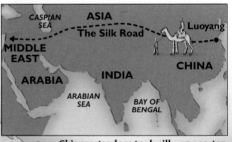

CASPIAN SEA
ASIA
The Silk Road
Luoyang
MIDDLE EAST
CHINA
ARABIA
INDIA
ARABIAN SEA
BAY OF BENGAL

Chinese traders took silk, paper, tea, lacquer and ceramics along the Silk Road.

THE MAYA IN AMERICA

The Maya, who lived in central America, entered their greatest period around AD250. They believed that their kings were gods and the kings celebrated their own importance by building cities and monuments for themselves. Mayan cities had splendid palaces for the king, open plazas, and courts for playing games with balls. Temples stood on top of stepped pyramids.

Around the year 1200, power shifted to the north and Mayapan and Chichen Itza became important. Mayapan was sacked in the 15th century and its people disappeared, but no one knows why this happened.

The Maya made wonderful pottery and stonework, and invented a form of picture writing. They believed that people should let blood to please the gods. People let their own blood at births, funerals and religious occasions. The Maya were once believed to be peaceful, but historians now think that rival kingdoms were often at war.

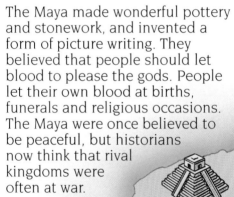

An 8th century Maya warrior.

THE MAYA EMPIRE

This map shows the great Maya Empire in central America and its most important cities.

•Mayapan
Coba
Uxmal
Chichen Itza
GULF OF MEXICO

CARIBBEAN SEA

In their cities, the Mayas built step pyramids with temples on top.

YUCATAN PENINSULA

N
W   E
S

MEXICO

SIERRA MADRE

Tikal

Palenque•

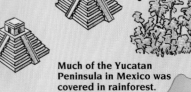

0   100   200 km
0   100 miles

Much of the Yucatan Peninsula in Mexico was covered in rainforest.

PACIFIC OCEAN

•Bonampak

Copan•

AFRICAN EMPIRES

During Europe's Middle Ages, fabulously rich empires existed in Africa. There were three great empires which rose and fell during this period. Ghana was the first, beginning around the year AD700. It was then absorbed into the larger Mali Empire, which was in turn replaced by the Songhai Empire, lasting until 1600.

The African Empires were rich because of their supply of gold. Arab traders bought salt from the Saharan salt mines, then carried it to towns in the southern Sahara, where they sold it for gold and slaves. Arab traders also converted many Africans to Islam.

Trade on the east coast of Africa also flourished. Gold, iron and ivory were sent from the town of Zimbabwe in the interior to the ports of Mombassa, Kilwa and Mogadishu.

One of Timbuktu's many mosques that impressed visitors to the city.

Timbuktu, in Mali, was one of the most impressive cities in Africa. It had busy markets, a great palace and several mosques. It also had a university.

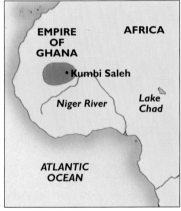

The fabulous Empire of Ghana in West Africa. It thrived from around AD700 to 1200.

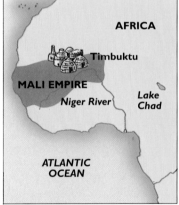

The Mali Empire, which existed from around 1200 to 1500, took over from the Empire of Ghana.

Later, the Songhai Empire took over from the Mali Empire. It existed from around 1350 to 1600.

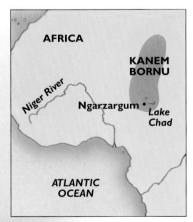

The Kingdom of Kanem Bornu developed separately. It thrived from around 800 to 1800.

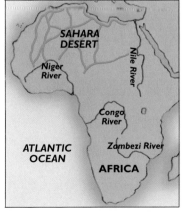

Saharan trade routes. Traders bought salt from the Sahara Desert mines and exchanged it for gold and slaves.

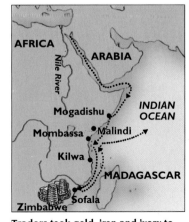

Traders took gold, iron and ivory to east African ports and shipped it to the Middle East, India and China.

TIME CHART

CHINA

AD618-907 T'ang Dynasty rules China.

7th-8th century Woodblock printing invented.

751 Chinese defeated by Turks at Battle of Taras.

9th century Gunpowder invented.

907-960 China is unsettled during the period of the Five Dynasties.

960 Sung Dynasty rules China.

c.1041 Movable type for printing is invented.

1125 Northern China captured from the Sung by nomads, who set up Ch'in Empire.

1279 Sung Dynasty in southern China is conquered by the Mongols.

AMERICA

c.AD200-850 Classical Period of Maya civilization in southern Yucatan.

750-1250 City of Mayapan flourishes.

c.800-1100 Growth of Post-Classical period of Maya civilization in northern Yucatan.

900-1100 The Toltecs flourish in Central America.

c.1460 Mayapan is sacked by unknown warriors.

c.1550 The Yucatan is conquered by the Spaniards.

AFRICA

c.AD700-1200 Kingdom of Ghana in West Africa.

c.800-1800 Kingdom of Kanem Bornu in West Africa.

c.1200-1500 Mali Empire thrives in West Africa.

c. 1270-1450 Zimbabwe is the capital of the Shona Empire in East Africa.

c.1350-1600 Songhai Empire thrives in West Africa.

FIND OUT MORE

America ▶ 40

China ◀ 48

Mongols ▶ 34

See above pages for more information.

EUROPE'S NEW AGE

During the Roman Empire, most citizens in Europe were Christian. Between AD400 and 500, barbarian invaders poured into Europe. These invaders were pagans, who did not believe in Christ. As they conquered Europe, they began to wipe out Christianity.

The 10th century German Emperor Otto I.

A farmhouse from Viking settlements of the 10th century.

A 10th century chapel, built for Charlemagne's palace in Aachen.

RETURN TO CHRISTIANITY

The Christian Church had been completely shaken by the barbarian invasions. By the 6th century, the wave of invasions settled down. The Church reorganized itself and set about the long, difficult and dangerous task of converting the barbarians to Christianity. There were three strongholds of the Church in Ireland, Rome and Constantinople. Each stronghold sent out men called missionaries, whose task it was to preach Christianity and convert the pagans.

By the 8th century, the barbarians had settled down into their own kingdoms and gradually they became Christians. Christianity was popular once more and the Church had succeeded in preserving the religion in Europe. It was also responsible for keeping alive the learning and skills that had been in danger of being lost during the barbarian invasions.

Missionary routes around Europe. The three different strongholds of Christianity sent out missionaries.

Missionaries from the Irish, or Celtic, Church spread Christianity in England and Scotland.

The Pope in Rome sent Christian missionaries to spread Christianity throughout Europe.

Missionaries from the Church in Constantinople spread Christianity in southeast Europe.

CHARLEMAGNE'S EMPIRE

One of the greatest kings in Europe in the 8th century was called Charles the Great, or Charlemagne, who was King of the Franks. After inheriting much of modern day France from his father, Charles set about fighting the pagans. Any captives that he took were forced to convert to Christianity and he built up the largest empire since the Romans. The Pope gave him the title "Emperor of the Romans".

After Charles's death, his empire was eventually divided into three – the Eastern, Middle and Western Frankish Kingdoms. The Middle Frankish Kingdom was eaten up by the others but in later years, the Eastern Frankish Kingdom covered what became modern day Germany. The Western Frankish Kingdom, which later developed into modern day France, was ruled by Charles's family until 987 when Hugh Capet became king.

A stained glass image of Charlemagne – "Emperor of the Romans".

Territory inherited by Charles between 768 and 771. It included much of what is now modern day France.

Territory conquered by Charles from 771 until his death in 814. His empire was the biggest in Europe since the Romans.

Charles's empire by 843. It had now been split into three – the Eastern, Middle and Western Frankish Kingdoms.

THE VIKING THREAT

Around 790, western Europe began to face a new pagan enemy – the Vikings. The Vikings came from Scandinavia. They were fishermen, farmers and merchants. They became rich, but their numbers grew, so there was not enough land for them all. Many took to the seas as pirates and raided coastal towns in search of loot. These raids were especially successful after the breakdown of the Frankish Empire.

The Vikings were adventurous seafarers. They sailed across oceans and up rivers, going as far as Constantinople on the edge of Europe and Baghdad in the Middle East. They sailed or rowed their boats along rivers as far as possible. Over land, the crew carried them or rolled them on logs. The Vikings traded with people along the way, exchanging iron, furs, bone and ivory for goods such as silver, spices and silks.

Some Vikings decided to stay in the areas they raided and fought to conquer territory. Over many years, they blended in with the local people. In eastern Europe, the native Slavs called the Vikings "Rus". The land that the Rus settled in is now called Russia. Other Vikings went farther afield to Iceland and Greenland in search of new homes. Some even reached North America, but settlements there failed to survive.

Viking routes across the North Sea and the sites of the Viking raids.

Viking trade and exploration routes across Europe, Asia and to America.

Settlements where the Vikings merged with local people.

FACING THE VIKINGS

Around this time, a number of events occurred in Europe which changed society. To combat the Vikings, European nobles began to employ well-armed, mounted soldiers. These soldiers could ride to the scene of a Viking raid quickly to defend their territory. Riders also began to use stirrups, which meant that they could withstand the shock of a charge without falling off their horses. Nobles fortified their towns and built strongholds made of earth and wood, where the local people could shelter in times of danger.

About 1100, Viking raids came to an end. By that time, a way of life had developed where people worked for the local lord in return for his protection. Because of this, many people also lost their freedom. This became the basis of the feudal system of the Middle Ages.

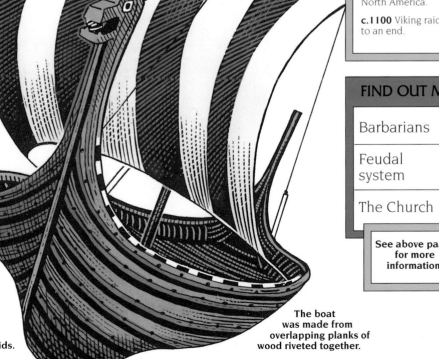

A Viking longship, which carried Vikings on their raids.

The boat was made from overlapping planks of wood riveted together.

FEUDAL EUROPE

In Europe, the years between 1050 to 1450 are called the Middle Ages. During the Middle Ages, society was organized in a way which we call the feudal system.

A monk and a nun of the Middle Ages.

A fully-armed knight of the Middle Ages.

As well as a sword and a shield, a knight carried a long spear called a lance.

THE FEUDAL SYSTEM

In feudal society, the king was the most powerful person. He owned the land, made the laws and led his army in battle. Nobles were given land and in return they obeyed and fought for him. Under the nobles served knights – warriors who fought for them or the king in return for land. The lowliest rank in society belonged to the peasants, who farmed the land in return for protection.

Europe in the Middle Ages, shown around the year 1300.

The knight's equipment was decorated with his own emblem, called a coat of arms.

Costume styles of the late 14th century – a king and queen.

A lord and lady.

A peasant, or serf.

THE HUNDRED YEARS' WAR

This was the longest of Europe's many wars in the Middle Ages. It began in 1339 because Edward III of England claimed he had a better right to the French throne than Philip of Valois. Despite great English victories and a couple of truces, the war dragged on.

A second successful English invasion was led by Henry V in 1415. Thirty years later, the French began pushing the English back until only Calais was left to them.

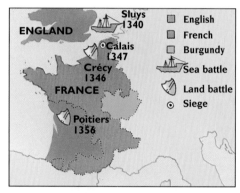

By 1360, the English controlled much of southwest France. They won decisive battles at Poitiers and Crécy.

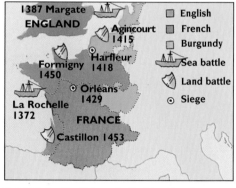

By 1429, the English controlled territory in southwest and northern France. Soon after this, they were pushed back.

THE CHURCH

In the Middle Ages, there were many monks and nuns, who devoted their whole lives to God. They lived in monasteries and nunneries where they prayed and worked. They gave to the poor, provided shelter for visitors and cared for the sick. To train churchmen, they also ran the first schools which later developed into the first universities in Europe.

Kings used priests in government because they could read and write. Many members of the Church became very powerful and the Church itself became rich.

Monks hand-decorated books with patterns like this.

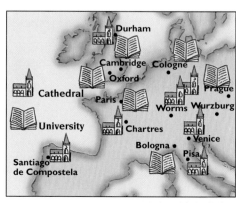

The first Christian universities and some great cathedrals that were founded in the Middle Ages.

TOWNS IN THE MIDDLE AGES

Trade increased in the Middle Ages and as it did so, towns grew up in Europe. Merchants and craftsmen banded together to form groups called guilds, which looked after their members and set standards of workmanship.

In some towns, the citizens became richer and wanted to be independent from their local lord. They paid him a sum of money for a charter, which gave them some self-government. In Germany and Italy, some cities became totally independent in this way. However, by and large, the rich still had all the power, which often led to revolts against them by the poor.

THE BLACK DEATH

In the 12th and 13th centuries, Europe became more prosperous. Then, at the start of the 14th century, bad weather caused harvests to fail. More ill luck followed when in 1347 a severe case of the bubonic plague, called the Black Death, arrived.

The plague came to Europe with the crew of a Genoese merchant ship returning from the Crimea in Russia. The crew were infested with the disease. It was carried by the fleas of black rats and it spread like wildfire across Europe. Over the next six years, it killed a third of the entire population, rich and poor alike.

People called the Flagellant Brotherhood thought that the plague was sent by God to punish them for their sins. They tried to stop the disease by whipping their bodies to punish themselves.

So many people died that the fields were left unfarmed, as there were not enough workers to tend the crops. Food prices were high and landowners kept wages low, which caused great hardship among the poor.

These hardships and other complaints against their masters sometimes led peasants to rebel. In 1358 there was the Jaquerie Uprising in France and in 1381 the Peasants' Revolt took place in England.

Although some groups of peasants managed to gain some freedom from their local lord, most revolts were stopped savagely. In most countries, the peasants still remained tied to their lord.

The seal on the charter of Bruges – a famous cloth-producing town in Belgium. Bruges is shown below.

In 1347, the plague was affecting the Byzantine Empire and southern Europe.

Within a year, it had spread north to cover the south and west of Europe.

By 1349, the plague had spread north again into Scandinavia.

Soon, central Europe and more of Scandinavia was affected.

By 1351, the plague spread north again into the area around the Baltic Sea.

By 1353, most areas in Europe were affected.

A merchant ship of the Middle Ages. Rats from a ship like this brought the plague to Europe.

FIND OUT MORE

The Church ◄ 26

Italy ► 37

See above pages for more information.

CLASH OF EMPIRES

After the western half of the Roman Empire collapsed, the eastern half survived for centuries. It became known as the Byzantine Empire and the city of Constantinople was its capital.

A Byzantine soldier.

An Ottoman soldier.

EAST MEETS WEST

Gradually, after the fall of Rome, the Byzantine Empire became more Greek in culture. Though constantly attacked by enemies, it was fabulously wealthy and held a key position at the crossroads of Europe and Asia. The reign of Basil II was a high point of Byzantine expansion. Basil managed to reconquer some of the territory that had belonged to the old Roman Empire.

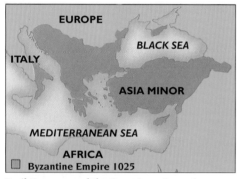

Basil II conquered the Georgians, Armenians, Bulgars and Arabs, bringing the empire to its height by 1025.

THE GREAT SCHISM

Relations between the Byzantines and their fellow Europeans were not always friendly because of differences in their religious beliefs. In 1054, the Church divided into the Roman Catholic and Orthodox Churches in a split called the Great Schism. In Constantinople, the Patriarch was head of the Orthodox Church, while in Rome, the Pope was head of the Catholic Church.

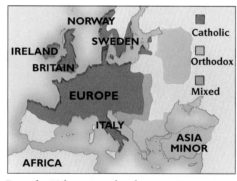

From the 11th century, the above areas were mainly influenced by the Roman Catholic and the Greek Orthodox Churches.

EMPIRE IN TROUBLE

Little by little, the Byzantine Empire shrank, as it was attacked from all sides. Then, a new enemy swept in from the east – the Seljuk Turks. In 1071, they won a great victory at Manzikert, capturing much territory.

A Byzantine chalice

The Seljuk Turks occupied a large area of Asia Minor in the 11th century and went on to rule most of the Middle East.

A mosaic of the Virgin Mary from the Byzantine church of Santa Sophia in Constantinople. When the Ottomans took over Constantinople (now Istanbul), the church became a Muslim mosque, as it still is today.

CHANGING EMPIRES

This map shows the Byzantine and Ottoman Empires. The Seljuk and Ottoman Turks nibbled away at the Byzantines until only Constantinople was left. Constantinople fell in 1453 and the Ottomans went on to capture a huge empire.

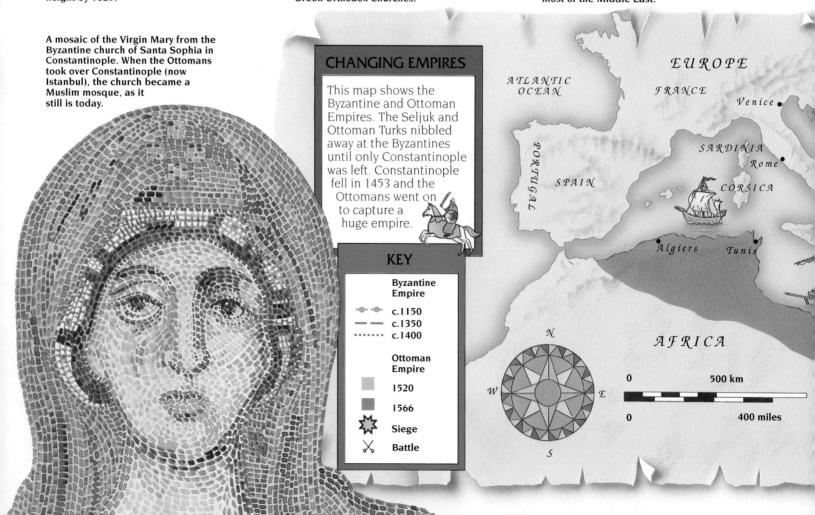

KEY

Byzantine Empire
- c.1150
- c.1350
- c.1400

Ottoman Empire
- 1520
- 1566
- Siege
- Battle

TIME CHART

976-1025 Reign of Byzantine Emperor Basil II.

1054 The Great Schism.

1071 Seljuk Turks win the Battle of Manzikert.

1301 Osman I sets up the Ottoman Empire.

1361 Byzantine Empire is reduced only to the city of Constantinople by the Ottomans.

1389 Ottomans win the Battle of Kossova.

1396 Bulgaria falls to the Ottomans.

1453 Constantinople falls to the Ottomans.

1512-20 Ottomans conquer Syria, Arabia and Egypt.

1520-66 Reign of Ottoman Sultan Suleiman I, the Magnificent.

1534 Ottomans conquer Persia.

1541 Hungary falls to the Ottomans.

1571 The Battle of Lepanto.

THE OTTOMANS

In the 13th century, groups of nomads fled west from Asia, driven by hordes of warriors called the Mongols. Among these nomads was a group of Muslims, known as the Ottoman Turks, who settled in Asia Minor from 1243. They carved out a province and in 1301, their leader proclaimed himself Sultan Osman I. From then on they advanced, conquering a huge empire.

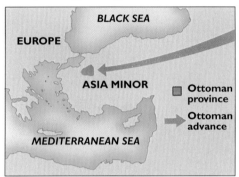

The Ottoman Turks originally came from around the region of Turkestan in west Asia. Their first province was in Asia Minor.

SULEIMAN I

The Byzantines were no match for the Ottomans. In 1453 Constantinople itself was captured. Ottoman territory grew and in 1520 Sultan Suleiman the Magnificent came to the throne. His reign saw the peak in Ottoman power.

Suleiman the Magnificent

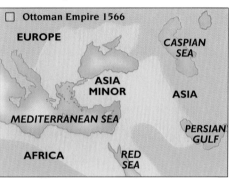

The Ottoman Empire reached its greatest extent by the death of Suleiman the Magnificent in 1566.

BATTLE OF LEPANTO

Over the centuries, the Poles, the Venetians, the French and the Hapsburgs, all fought against the Ottomans, but to little advantage. Then in 1571 the combined fleet of the Holy League (Spain, Venice, Genoa and the Papal States) crushed the Ottomans in a sea battle at Lepanto. This broke their domination of the Mediterranean and from then on the Ottoman Empire slowly declined.

The Battle of Lepanto, between the Holy League and the Ottoman Turks took place off the coast of Greece, in an inlet of the Mediterranean Sea.

The Battle of Lepanto was the last great battle to be fought at sea using oar-powered galleys, like the one shown below.

This plan shows how the fleets of the Holy League and the Ottoman Turks lined up for battle at the Battle of Lepanto.

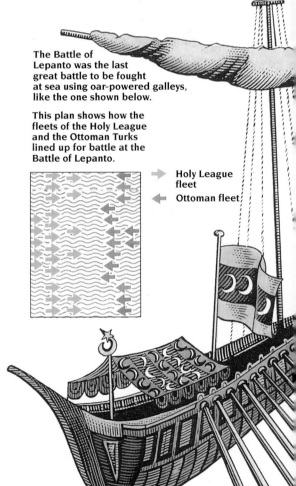

→ Holy League fleet

← Ottoman fleet

THE CRUSADES

Palestine, or the Holy Land, had been ruled by Muslims since the 7th century. Christians had been able to go on pilgrimages there to visit the area where Christ lived, but in the 11th century Seljuk Turks conquered the Holy Land and made it difficult and dangerous for Christians to enter.

The Krak de Chevaliers – a Crusader castle guarding the Holy Land.

Pope Urban II, who first urged people of Europe to go on a crusade.

THE CALL TO ARMS

Saladin – the Muslim leader who beat back the Third Crusade.

In 1095, Pope Urban II preached a sermon at Clermont in France. He urged people to go on a crusade, or holy war, to free the Holy Land from the Turks. Urban said that if they died on the way, their sins would be forgiven and they would go to heaven. Ordinary people from all over Europe swore to go, crying "God wills it!" Soon after this, a disorganized band of peasants and adventurers set out on the People's Crusade. However, they were killed or died of disease and hunger long before they got there.

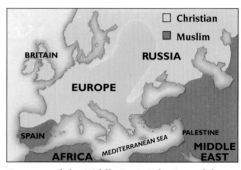

Europe and the Middle East at the time of the First Crusade in the late 11th century.

TO THE HOLY LAND

The First Crusade of noblemen and soldiers set out in 1096. It took three years for them to reach Jerusalem, but in an all-out attack in 1099, they captured the city. The area captured by the Crusaders was called Outremer. Many Crusaders returned to Europe, which left Outremer short of soldiers to protect it. The Christians were now outnumbered, and the Muslims united to drive them out.

The Muslims captured Edessa and a Second Crusade failed. Then the Muslims became even stronger under a leader called Saladin, who recaptured Jerusalem. A Third Crusade then set out led by the English, German and French Kings. The Crusaders won many battles, but not Jerusalem. A Fourth Crusade only got as far as Constantinople, where its members sacked the city, stealing its treasures. Many knights went on the Crusades to become rich, as well as for religious reasons.

The Muslims, also known as Saracens, rode lightweight, fast horses for a quick attack.

Muslim fighters wore fabric-covered chainmail to protect them.

The First Crusade of 1096-99. Knights rode to the Holy Land via Constantinople.

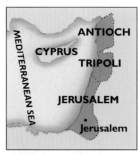
The Crusader kingdoms, known as Outremer, in the 12th century.

The Second Crusade of 1147-49. From Constantinople, the Crusaders sailed to Acre.

The Third Crusade of 1189-92, led by the English, French and German kings.

The Fourth Crusade of 1202-04. The knights sacked Constantinople.

THE KNIGHTS

During the Crusades, new religious orders were founded. Members took the same vows as monks – poverty, chastity and obedience. That is, they agreed to give up their possessions, never to marry and to obey their superiors. These men were also knights, who promised to fight to defend the Holy Land. The leading orders were the Knights Templars, the Knights of St. John and the Teutonic Knights.

Even after they were driven out of the Holy Land by Muslims, some orders of crusader knights survived. The Knights of St. John still occupied Rhodes until 1523, when they transferred to the island of Malta.

The emblem of the Knights of St. John.

The emblem of the Knights Templar.

The emblem of the Teutonic Knights.

MORE CRUSADES

In 1212, thousands of European children followed a shepherd boy on a crusade that became known as the Children's Crusade. They believed that God would perform miracles so they could recapture Jerusalem. Merchants at Marseilles in France offered to take the children in their ships to the Holy Land. Instead, however, they took them to Alexandria in Egypt and sold them as slaves.

During the rest of the 13th century, the Fifth, Sixth and Seventh Crusades all set out for the Holy Land. Holy Roman Emperor Frederick II managed to win back Jerusalem by treaty, but this was only temporarily. The Muslims continued to reconquer the Christian states and at last in 1291, Acre, the last Christian stronghold, fell.

TIME CHART

1071 Seljuk Turks defeat the Byzantines at the Battle of Manzikert.

1085-1492 The Reconquest of Spain by Christians.

1095 Byzantine Emperor appeals to Pope Urban II.

1096 Pope Urban II launches First Crusade. Peter the Hermit sets out on the People's Crusade.

1096-99 First Crusade.

1099 Christians capture Jerusalem.

1144 Muslims capture Edessa.

1147-49 Second Crusade.

1187 Saladin defeats Christians at Hattin and captures Jerusalem.

1189-92 Third Crusade.

1202-04 Fourth Crusade.

1204 Constantinople sacked by crusaders.

1209-29 Crusade against the Albigensians in southern France.

1212 Children's Crusade.

1228-29 Fifth Crusade.

1248-54 Sixth Crusade.

1270 Seventh Crusade.

1291 Fall of Acre – the last Christian stronghold.

CRUSADES OUTSIDE THE HOLY LAND

The idea of a crusade spread from the Holy Land to other areas. The Pope encouraged crusades against political enemies and heretics. Among these was a group called the Albigensians in southern France. The Albigensians were heretics, which means that they disagreed with some of the teachings of the Catholic Church. French nobles wiped them out in a religious war.

In Spain and Portugal, Christians fought a crusade against Muslims from North Africa, called the Moors, who had occupied nearly all of Spain and Portugal since the 8th century. From 1085, Christians spread slowly south during a period which is known as the Reconquest. Eventually, in 1492, the last Moorish kingdom was captured by King Ferdinand and Queen Isabella of Spain. This kingdom, Granada, is still a province of Spain today.

The King of England – Richard I, the Lionheart. He was one of the leaders of the Third Crusade.

FIND OUT MORE

Spain	▶ 40
Turks	◀ 30

See above pages for more information.

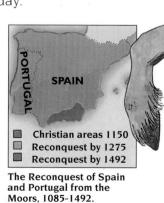

The crusade against the Albigensians in France from 1209-29.

FRANCE

Dijon •

Toulouse •

Avignon

The Reconquest of Spain and Portugal from the Moors, 1085-1492.

PORTUGAL

SPAIN

■ Christian areas 1150
□ Reconquest by 1275
■ Reconquest by 1492

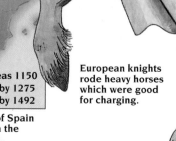

European knights rode heavy horses which were good for charging.

Richard wore the royal coat of arms on his shield.

The Mongols were fierce soldiers. Men were trained to fight on horseback.

THE MONGOLS

The Mongols lived in the Steppes of Central Asia – great grassy plains between Hungary and Mongolia. They were nomads, who herded horses and sheep for their living. They were always on the move, in search of new grazing land for their animals. They lived in movable, felt tents, called yurts.

A large, decorated Mongol yurt.

GENGHIS KHAN

Around 1162, a boy called Temujin was born into a noble Mongol family. Temujin meant "blacksmith". When he was nine, his father was murdered by rivals and Temujin had to be very quick-witted to survive his father's enemies.

When he grew up, Temujin made daring raids on other tribes, and he began to attract many followers. Men from other tribes swore oaths to be his loyal companion or *noker*.

Temujin became more and more successful and gradually brought all the different Mongol tribes under his control. In 1206, the tribes met together and made him the Supreme Ruler or "Genghis Khan". He was the first to unite the Mongol tribes under one leader. As leader, Genghis Khan controlled all the armies of the other tribes.

The Mongol homeland, northwest of China. In the 11th century, the Mongols had not conquered any territory farther afield.

The Mongol Empire at the death of Genghis Khan in 1227. During his lifetime, Genghis had occupied parts of China and most of Asia.

THE MAKING OF AN EMPIRE

Genghis invaded northern China and also took Khwarazm-Shah (modern Iran and Afghanistan). To rule his empire, he is said to have issued the Great Yasa – laws for his subjects to obey. The Mongols had no alphabet, so he adopted that of the Uighur Turks. Genghis also set up a network of stage posts, so that relay riders could take messages swiftly across the empire.

Genghis Khan, the first great Mongol ruler.

Genghis returned home to Mongolia in 1223 and died four years later. The empire he created survived. By 1225, the Mongols ruled most of Asia. In their conquests, the Mongols gained an evil reputation. They massacred people and destroyed whole cities. If people submitted instantly, however, the Mongols spared them.

Batu, who was a grandson of Genghis, swept west through Russia. He nearly reached Vienna, but then the Great Khan Ogedei died and the army was called back to Mongolia.

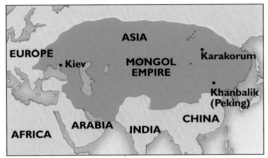

Hulegu, another grandson of Genghis, conquered Persia and Syria in 1253. This territory became known as Il Khanate.

KUBLAI KHAN'S EMPIRE

The empire continued to grow under Ghengis's sons and grandsons. In the west, the Mongols advanced almost to Vienna. In the east, the conquest of China was completed by Kublai Khan, Genghis's grandson, when the Sung Empire fell in 1279. Kublai Khan settled in China with his capital in Peking (Beijing). His court was magnificent, but after his death, the Chinese drove out the Mongols in 1368.

The Mongols captured Sung China in 1279. The empire was now at its greatest extent. It was split into Khanates, ruled by Kublai's deputies.

MARCO POLO

In the 13th century, trade routes in Asia were controlled by the Mongols. In 1271, two Venetians, Nicolo and Maffeo Polo, went on their second journey to Asia, taking Nicolo's son Marco. They visited Kublai Khan's court, and stayed in Asia for 20 years.

Marco later told the story of his travels around Kublai Khan's empire. The story was written down and became one of the most popular of the Middle Ages.

The Polos meeting Kublai Khan. They presented him with gifts.

TIME CHART

1162 Temujin born in Mongolia.

1206 Temujin becomes Ghengis Khan and attacks China.

1225 Genghis Khan masters most of Asia.

1227 Genghis Khan dies.

1235 Mongols begin to invade Russia and Eastern Europe.

1241 Mongols withdraw from Western Europe.

1260-94 Kublai Khan is the Mongol Emperor.

1260 Mongols advance into Middle East. Halted by Battle of Ain Jalut.

1271-95 Marco Polo travels in Asia.

1274 Mongols fail to invade Japan.

1279 Conquest of China completed.

1281 Second Mongol invasion of Japan fails.

1297 Marco Polo is captured and imprisoned by the Genoese. He begins to tell the story of his travels, which is written down by a fellow prisoner.

1369-1405 Tamerlane is in power.

1398 Tamerlane attacks Delhi in India.

1504-30 Babur founds the Mogul Empire.

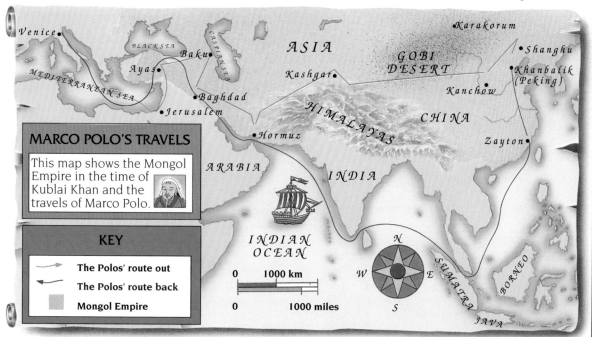

MARCO POLO'S TRAVELS

This map shows the Mongol Empire in the time of Kublai Khan and the travels of Marco Polo.

KEY

→ The Polos' route out

← The Polos' route back

▨ Mongol Empire

TAMERLANE

After Kublai Khan died, the empire fell apart. Then in 1360, a descendant of his, known as Tamerlane, conquered a new Mongol Empire. He took land in Persia, Russia and India. However, after he died in 1405, his empire did not last long.

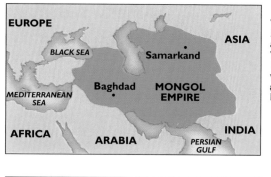

The extent of the Mongol Empire at the death of Tamerlane in 1405. Tamerlane was the last great Mongol Emperor.

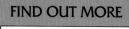

See above pages for more information.

THE MOGUL EMPIRE

In the late 15th century, part of the Mongol Empire was taken over by the Turks. A Mongol prince called Babur was forced to flee from the Turks to Afghanistan.

Babur soon began to conquer new territory and by 1504, he was in control of Kabul. He then captured Delhi in 1526. He and his descendants, known as the Moguls, created a fabulous empire in India. It survived until the 18th century, when conflicts between the Muslim Moguls and their Hindu subjects helped the empire to collapse.

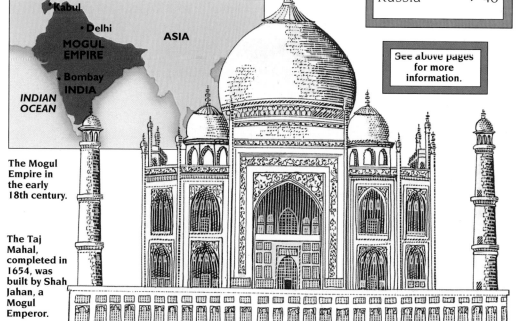

The Mogul Empire in the early 18th century.

The Taj Mahal, completed in 1654, was built by Shah Jahan, a Mogul Emperor.

THE RENAISSANCE

In Europe, in the late 14th to 16th centuries, there was a revival of interest in the art, architecture and learning of Ancient Greece and Rome. This movement is known as the Renaissance, which means "rebirth".

An early printing press.

Gutenberg's press was adapted from a cheese or wine press. It could print up to 300 sheets a day.

Part of a page from Gutenberg's printed Bible. Decorated patterns were painted on by hand.

THE RENAISSANCE BEGINS

In the Middle Ages, art and literature were intended to make people think about God. In Italy in the 14th century, these ideas began to change. The rebirth of interest in Ancient Greece and Rome changed the way people saw the world. Religion continued to be vital, but artists and thinkers now began to base their work on human life and the events around them. A new spirit of learning and questioning was born.

PRINTING

In 1453, a German goldsmith, Johannes Gutenberg, invented the printing press. Until then, all books were painstakingly hand-copied, so they were rare and expensive. Now, using movable metal letters to make blocks of type, printers produced hundreds of identical copies quickly and cheaply. Paper was becoming cheaper too, and so the price of books fell.

At first, most books were printed in Latin, and many were on religious subjects. But soon many books on other topics were printed as well. Printed materials carried the ideas of the Reformation quickly throughout Europe.

SCULPTURE

Studying the statues of Greece and Rome, sculptors studied the human body. They carved religious subjects, scenes from stories and the famous men and women of their day.

These two sculptures show the change in art during the Renaissance. Medieval carvings were often full of character and charm, but they lacked the realism of later works, like the *Pietà* by Michelangelo.

The *Pietà*, or "Devotion", shows Mary cradling the body of her son, Jesus.

Medieval carving (above) of a crusader and his wife.

Print shops in 1471. The first press was set up in Mainz in Germany.

By 1500 there were 226 presses throughout Europe.

SCIENCE

People became curious about the world. Scientists studied medicine, physics, chemistry and biology. Astronomers Copernicus and Galileo challenged the belief that the Earth was at the heart of the universe, and showed that the Earth revolves around the Sun.

ARCHITECTURE

Architects also copied the style of Ancient Greece and Rome. They designed churches, public buildings, palaces and houses with columns, rounded arches and central domes. Two important architects of the time were Andrea Palladio and Donato Bramante.

PAINTING

During the Renaissance, artists studied the human body and how it moved, as well as the use of perspective. They began to paint life-like people in realistic backgrounds. They painted pictures of recent events, scenes from the legends of Ancient Greece and Rome, and portraits of rich people.

LITERATURE

Scholars studied Greek and Roman literature and used classical ideas when writing in their own languages. There was a flowering of poetry and drama. In England, people flocked to see Shakespeare's plays at the new Globe Theatre.

RENAISSANCE MEN AND WOMEN

During the Renaissance, men from rich families received a magnificent education in the arts and sciences. They had to be well-mannered and brave, and they were expected to be good swordsmen, riders, poets and musicians. Unsurprisingly, not many men could live up to this ideal. Rich women, like Queen Elizabeth I of England and Marguerite of Navarre, sister of the French king, received a good education too.

Popes, kings and men and women of the nobility were interested in the new arts. They became patrons, winning fame and glory by paying for work by great artists and scholars. The Medici family of Florence, for instance, paid for a great library, chapels and palaces, as well as paintings and sculptures by Michelangelo and many other artists.

Michelangelo designed this graceful dome to tower over Rome's skyline.

In 1506 Pope Julius II commissioned St. Peter's cathedral in Rome.

An engraving of Copernicus's theory of the universe. The Sun is in the middle. The Church disapproved of scientists like Copernicus who questioned its teachings. It tried to stop him publishing his ideas.

TIME CHART

1418 Brunelleschi designs the dome of Florence Cathedral.

1453 Gutenburg invents the first printing press in Mainz, Germany.

1467-1536 Life of Erasmus, greatest scholar of the Renaissance.

1468-92 Lorenzo de Medici, patron of the arts, rules Florence.

1503-07 Leonardo da Vinci paints the *Mona Lisa*.

1475-1564 Life of Michelangelo Buonarroti.

1509 Venice suffers defeat by the French and Genoese.

1519-56 Reign of Holy Roman Emperor Charles V.

1543 Copernicus publishes his theories of the universe.

1564-1642 Life of astronomer Galileo Galilei.

1564-1616 Life of playwright William Shakespeare.

FIND OUT MORE

Middle Ages ◄ 28

Reformation ► 42

See above pages for more information.

ITALY AND THE HOLY ROMAN EMPIRE

The Pope, the powerful head of the Catholic Church, ruled the Papal States in Italy. The Popes and the Holy Roman Emperors had often clashed over power. This sometimes led to war.

The power of the Popes was weakened during the Renaissance by the new religious ideas of the Reformation.

During the Renaissance, Italy was a place of great turmoil. It was split up into several kingdoms and many smaller independent states. Part of northern Italy also belonged to the Holy Roman Empire.

Rulers struggled ruthlessly for power. Machiavelli's famous book, *The Prince*, tells of the politics of the day.

In 1519, Charles V was elected Holy Roman Emperor. He was a member of the Hapsburg family, which dominated Europe.

Charles had inherited the throne of Spain, already immensely wealthy because of its New World colonies. Under his rule, the Holy Roman Empire became united and powerful.

Some cities had grown rich through trade and became independent states. Strong cities, such as Venice, swallowed up weaker ones around them.

As a result these cities, known as city-states, often fought over territory. Vicious mercenary soldiers, called *condottieri*, fought for whoever paid them.

The Papal States around the year 1500. The Pope's capital was Rome.

Italy in the year 1500. By then, the Renaissance was well under way.

Charles V ruled both the Holy Roman Empire and the Spanish Empire.

Venetian territory around 1500. Its empire had spread as far as Crete.

EXPLORING THE WORLD

From very early times, people had always explored new places to find homes, to meet people for trading purposes, or simply out of curiosity for the unknown. From the 1450s, European sailors set out on the first great voyages to India and also to America. Over the coming centuries, these journeys were to lead to explorations of the whole world.

Ibn Battuta, the 14th century Arab explorer.

Cook's chronometer – an important aid to navigation. It was the first clock that could keep going for the time of an around-the-world voyage.

EARLY EXPLORERS

The Polynesians explored around the Pacific Ocean, colonizing many of the islands there by the 11th century AD. By the 15th century, Arab traders had explored the east coast of Africa and had journeyed to India and China. Ibn Battuta was the most famous Arab explorer, undertaking several journeys across Asia. The Chinese also explored and had been sailing to Africa since the 9th century.

In the Middle East, European traders bought luxury goods which originally came from the East, such as silks and spices. However, this trade became increasingly difficult because of the hostility of the Turks. By the 15th century, Europeans were wondering if it was possible to reach the east by sea and they began to try to find a route.

Ibn Battuta's travels in the 14th century. Ibn Battuta was born in Tangiers, Africa, but spent most of his life on his travels or living in distant places.

The journeys of Chinese explorers Fa Hsien (4th century AD) and Hsuan Tsang (7th century AD). They improved Chinese knowledge of India and Asia.

HENRY THE NAVIGATOR

In the early 15th century, Prince Henry of Portugal, known as "Henry the Navigator" was sure that ships could sail around Africa to reach Asia. So, he set up a community in Sagres to build better ships and make better maps and navigation equipment.

Henry's captains sailed from Sagres along the African coast, going farther and farther south each time.

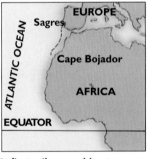

At first sailors would not go around Cape Bojador in Africa. They thought that at the Equator, the Sun was so close to the Earth that the sea boiled and the land was on fire. Gil Eannes was the first to sail around it in 1434.

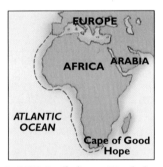

In 1487, Bartholomeu Dias led an expedition from Portugal to sail around the southern tip of Africa. By luck they managed it and on their return, the King of Portugal named it the Cape of Good Hope.

In 1497, another Portuguese captain, called Vasco da Gama, set off around Africa. He sailed up the East African coast, where he stopped to pick up supplies. He then sailed across the Indian Ocean to India.

THE WAY WEST

Some people believed that the world was flat, but others thought differently. One of them, Christopher Columbus, believed that the world was round and that it would be quicker to reach the east by sailing west across the Atlantic. He did not realize that America lay in the way. Other sailors kept trying the eastern route. Then in 1492 King Ferdinand and Queen Isabella of Spain agreed to pay for Columbus to try his plan. He set out to prove his theory.

After two and a half months at sea, Columbus landed in the West Indies, off the coast of America. He thought that he had reached islands in the Indian Ocean and that is why they became known as the Indies. He did not know he had discovered America.

The Spaniards and the Portuguese became great rivals for new land. In 1494 the Pope fixed a treaty line between them – the Treaty of Tordesillas. The Portuguese were to own land discovered east of the line and the Spaniards to the west of it.

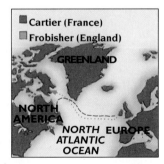

Other nations took no notice of the Treaty of Tordesillas, or the claims of Spain and Portugal. The Dutch, English and French all claimed land for themselves. Ships from both France and England sailed west also to find a passage to the east.

INTO THE UNKNOWN

Sailing into unknown seas was dangerous. Sailors risked death from shipwreck or illness, caused by poor food and appalling conditions. As well as believing that the sea boiled near the Equator, people imagined that huge monsters lurked beneath the waves and that the people in lands far away would look like strange freaks. People drew pictures of the natives and monsters they imagined lived in foreign lands.

A "sea-devil" – an imaginary monster.

Imaginary people from foreign lands.

AROUND THE WORLD

Exploring America (known as the New World) soon led to the first trip all the way around the world, or circumnavigation. This was achieved by a Portuguese captain, called Ferdinand Magellan, who was in the service of the King of Spain. He believed that he could reach the east by sailing around the tip of South America. In 1519 he set out to prove it.

The second circumnavigation was not achieved until 58 years later, by the Englishman Francis Drake.

At the tip of South America, Magellan found a passage to the Pacific Ocean, now called the Straits of Magellan. His party sailed around the world home to Spain, but Magellan was killed in the Philippines.

At the tip of South America, Magellan's crew had sighted land which they called Tierra del Fuego ("land of fire"). They were not sure whether this was an island or the tip of a great southern continent.

In 1577, Francis Drake was sent out by the Elizabeth I of England to find out if Tierra del Fuego was a new continent. Drake proved that Tierra del Fuego was an island and then sailed on around the world.

THE SOUTHERN SEAS

The Dutch were the first Europeans to reach Australia. The first, Willem Jantszoon, reached the north coast in 1606. In 1642, another Dutchman, Abel Tasman, sighted the island now known as Tasmania.

Interest in Australia then stopped. It was another hundred years before Englishman James Cook made three great voyages to Australia and around the Pacific Ocean.

Between 1642 and 1643, Abel Tasman sighted Tasmania (which he named Van Dieman's Land) and sailed on to New Zealand. He also stopped at the islands of Tonga and Fiji.

Cook's first voyage took place from 1768 to 1771. On board were scientists and artists to record his findings. He named his landing spot, on the east coast of Australia, Botany Bay.

On Cook's third voyage, he became involved in a dispute and was killed by natives on the Sandwich Islands (now Hawaii).

TIME CHART

1304-77 Life of Ibn Battuta.

1419 Henry the Navigator sets up a community in Sagres, Portugal.

1434 Gil Eannes sails past Cape Bojador.

1492 Columbus reaches the West Indies.

1494 Treaty of Tordesillas.

1497 Da Gama sails from Portugal to India. John Cabot in the service of the King of England reaches Newfoundland.

1499-1502 Amerigo Vespucci, after whom America is named, sails around America.

1519-21 Cortes conquers Aztec Empire in Central America.

1519-22 Magellan leads first voyage around the world.

1531-34 Pizarro conquers Inca Empire in South America.

1577-80 Drake sails around the world.

1580 Portugal is united with Spain.

1642 Tasman sails around Australia.

1768-71 Cook's first voyage to Australia.

1770 Cook lands in Botany Bay, Australia.

1772-75 Cook's second voyage. He reaches Easter Island – the farthest south yet reached by a European.

1776-79 Cook's third voyage. He is killed in Hawaii.

FIND OUT MORE

Europe   ◀ 36

The Americas ▶ 40

See above pages for more information.

Columbus's ship was a Portuguese caravel called the *Santa Maria*. The first voyages of discovery were made in caravels.

THE NEW WORLD

In the 16th century, when Europeans first journeyed to the Americas, the lives of the native Americans were soon to change forever. Europeans were eager to make the most of this new continent – the New World.

A Spanish conquistador.

THE AZTECS

In the 15th century, the Aztecs in Central America expanded from their capital, Tenochtitlan. They created an empire by conquering surrounding tribes. The Aztecs built glorious cities with temples, open squares or plazas, and courts where they played a ritual ball game.

The Aztecs were continually at war to find victims for human sacrifice. They believed that without this sacrifice, the sun god would die.

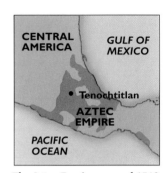

The Aztec Empire, around 1519. Tenochtitlan was founded in the early 14th century.

The Aztec god Tonatiuh.

The Incas did not write, but tied knots in strings, called quipu, to make messages.

THE INCAS

In the 15th century, the Incas in South America began to expand from their capital of Cuzco. Believed by his people to be half-god, half-human, the ninth king Pachacuti conquered a huge empire. Everyone in the empire had to work in accordance with their rank and ability. In return, the orphans, the sick and the elderly were cared for.

The Incas built good roads across the difficult, rough land of their empire. They were expert stonemasons, and also built impressive public buildings. Most people earned their living by farming.

The Inca Empire in 1525, during the reign of the god-king Huayna Capac.

THE ARRIVAL OF THE SPANIARDS

After the arrival of Columbus in America, the first Europeans to explore were the Spaniards. The Spanish conquerors, known as conquistadors, were greedy for the immense riches of the Aztec and Inca Empires. Between 1519 and 1522, an expedition led by Hernan Cortes conquered the Aztecs and killed their god-king Montezuma II. The Spaniards were helped by local tribes who hated the Aztecs for their cruelty. Then in 1533, conquistadors led by Francisco Pizarro overthrew the Incas too. Spain became the richest nation in Europe.

A Spanish coin, called a doubloon, made from South American gold.

The gold handle of a ceremonial knife from the Andes.

An Aztec chest ornament, made from turquoise, in the shape of a serpent.

Cortes's route from the West Indies to the Aztec Empire, 1519 to 1522.

Pizarro's route from the coast to the Inca Empire, 1532 to 1533.

NORTH AMERICA

In North America, there were dozens of Indian tribes, living varied lifestyles. The Indians of the southwest were farmers, living in stone villages, or pueblos. Farther north there too were farmers, and people who hunted and gathered their food, and fishermen. Tribes had their own languages and cultures, and were often at war with one another.

Before Europeans arrived, Indians did not ride horses. Horses were brought to America by the Spaniards.

NORTH AMERICAN INDIANS

Before Europeans arrived, there were dozens of Indian tribes. This map shows the main ones.

TIME CHART

1437-71 Pachacuti extends the Inca Empire.

1492 Columbus arrives in the West Indies.

1497-98 An Italian, called Cabot, reaches Newfoundland in North America on behalf of the English.

1502-20 Reign of Aztec god-king Montezuma II.

1519-21 Cortes conquers the Aztecs.

1532-33 Pizarro conquers the Incas.

1540-41 New Mexico is colonized for the Spaniards by Francisco Vazquez de Coronado.

1542-45 Laws are introduced by the Spaniards to protect American Indians.

1584 Roanoke in Virginia becomes the first English colony to be set up in North America. It fails.

1603 First French governor arrives in Canada.

1604 Acadia, the first French colony, is set up.

1607 Jamestown, the first permanent British settlement, is set up.

1616 The Dutch set up a colony called New Netherlands.

1620 A group called the Pilgrims from England land at Plymouth Rock in Massachusetts.

1625 New Amsterdam is founded by the Dutch.

1632 English Catholics seeking religious freedom set up the colony of Maryland.

1667 The Dutch lose their colonies to the English. New Amsterdam becomes New York.

1680 Spanish farmers are massacred by Pueblo Indians in New Mexico.

1682 The French set up the Louisiana Territory. Englishman William Penn founds the city of Philadelphia and the Quaker colony of Pennsylvania.

Indians from the Great Plains area of North America, as seen by a 19th century artist.

THE COLONIES

In the late 16th century, Europeans arrived in North America. They settled in colonies and fought each other to gain territory. Soon there were Spanish, English, French and Dutch colonies.

Some Indians resisted the new settlers and Europeans offered rewards in return for killing them. At other times, both the French and the English used Indians to fight their wars against each other.

Spanish colonies around the Caribbean in the 17th century.

English colonies in America in the 17th century. Their first colony was Jamestown.

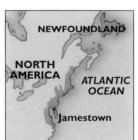

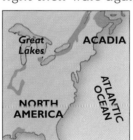

French colonies in America in the 17th century. Their first settlement was Acadia.

Dutch colonies in the Americas in the 17th century.

FREEDOM IN AMERICA

Not all Europeans came to America to seek their fortunes. Many came to escape from the religious troubles that tore Europe apart in the 16th and 17th centuries. Some of the first English settlers to arrive in America were a group of Protestants called the Pilgrims. They arrived in Massachusetts in 1620 aboard their ship *The Mayflower*. They came to America so that they could worship freely and run their lives how they wished.

Members of the Pilgrims.

FIND OUT MORE

Explorers	◄	38
Religion	►	42
USA	►	60
Wars in Europe	►	44

See above pages for more information.

THE REFORMATION

In early 16th century Europe, many people felt that the Roman Catholic Church was in urgent need of reform. Popes were criticized for their interest in wealth, pleasure and power and many priests were greedy and lazy. As a result, some people began to criticize the Church.

Leo X who was Pope during the start of the Reformation.

Martin Luther – his criticisms led to a split in the Christian Church.

MARTIN LUTHER

In 1517, a young monk named Martin Luther pinned a document to a church door in Wittenburg in Germany. Called the Ninety Five Theses, it called for a discussion about the Church. Luther particularly objected to the sale of indulgences – certificates which pardoned people's sins. The Pope condemned Luther, but many Germans supported him.

Luther's ideas were made public when he pinned them to a church door.

People whose beliefs went against those of the Church were known as heretics and could be burned at the stake. However Luther had powerful friends who protected him from the Pope and the Holy Roman Emperor, Charles V. The followers of Luther and other reformers became known as Protestants. This movement is called the Reformation because of people's desire to reform the Catholic Church.

Luther's ideas spread quickly, helped by new printing presses like the one above.

□ Protestant
□ Catholic/ Protestant
□ Orthodox/ Islam
□ Catholic

By 1570, Protestantism had spread across Europe and soon separated into different branches. Spain and Italy remained Catholic strongholds.

THE CHURCH IN ENGLAND

In 1528, King Henry VIII of England decided to ask the Pope for a divorce from his wife, Catherine of Aragon. Henry wanted a new wife because Catherine had only given him a daughter and Henry believed that he needed a son to be king after him. The Pope refused to do this because he was in an awkward position – a divorce would offend Catherine's nephew, Holy Roman Emperor Charles V. In order to get his divorce, Henry made himself head of the Church in England and closed down the monasteries. The Church of England later became fully Protestant in the reign of Henry's son.

CATHOLICS FIGHT BACK

In 1534, a powerful religious order, called the Society of Jesus, or the Jesuits, was set up to convert people in America and Asia to Christianity and to win Protestants back to the Catholic Church. Then in 1545, the Catholic Church, realizing that it was still under attack from Protestantism, called the Council of Trent to establish its beliefs and find ways to reconvert Protestants. This revival of Catholicism is called the Counter Reformation.

Both Protestants and Catholics were fully prepared to persecute, torture and execute each other in the name of their religion.

The Holy Roman Emperor Charles V (also Charles I of Spain). He was a Catholic and the nephew of Henry VIII's wife Catherine of Aragon.

Here, Charles is dressed in his imperial regalia as the Holy Roman Emperor.

RELIGIOUS WARS

In Europe in the 16th century, people believed passionately that they would only go to heaven if they followed what they believed was the true faith. As a result, for over 150 years Europe was torn apart by religious wars. Political alliances tended to be made between countries that followed the same religion (though not always) and differences in religious belief was often the major cause of wars, including civil wars.

English playing cards of the 17th century, telling the story of the English defeat of the Spanish fleet.

FRANCE

France had a large number of Protestants known as the Huguenots, among whom were many of France's nobility. From 1562 to 1598, bitter civil wars were fought and in 1572, 20,000 Huguenots were killed by Catholics at the Massacre of St. Bartholomew's Eve. The civil wars ended when the Huguenot Henry IV of Navarre became King of France. Henry was converted to Catholicism but he granted Huguenots the freedom of worship. This was later withdrawn.

Areas under Huguenot control in France in the late 16th century.

THE NETHERLANDS

In the 16th century, the Netherlands were part of the Spanish Empire. Philip II of Spain tried to impose absolute rule over the Dutch and he persecuted Protestants. In 1566 the Dutch rebelled and two years later, war broke out. It seemed an impossible task – a few tiny provinces against Spain, the mightiest nation in Europe. However in 1648, seven provinces did gain independence and they became known as the United Provinces.

In 1648, part of the Netherlands became independent from Spain.

DEFEAT FOR SPAIN

Though he once thought of marrying Protestant Elizabeth I of Engand, Philip II of Spain came to see her as one of his greatest enemies. So, in 1588, he tried to invade England. He sent a fleet of ships, called the Armada, to carry his soldiers from the Netherlands to England. However, Philip's plan failed when the skill of the English navy and bad weather combined to wreck the fleet. Many of the ships sank in British waters.

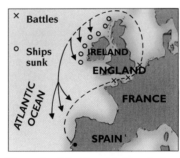

The route of the Spanish Armada in 1588.

TIME CHART

1478 The Spaniards revive the Inquisition to persecute Jews and Muslims who pretended to be Christians for safety, but secrectly followed their own religions.

1483-1546 Life of Martin Luther, Protestant reformer.

1517 Luther issues his Ninety Five Theses, protesting against the failings of the Church.

1519-56 Reign of Charles V, Holy Roman Emperor.

1522-25 A series of Protestant rebellions takes place in the Holy Roman Empire.

1534 Henry VIII becomes Supreme Head of the English Church.

1545-63 The Council of Trent defines the doctrines of the Catholic Church, in response to the rise in Protestantism.

1555 Emperor Charles V gives tolerance to Lutherans in the Religious Peace of Augsburg, which allows them to follow their own religion.

1556-98 Reign of Philip II, King of Spain.

1558-1603 Reign of Elizabeth I, Queen of England.

1562-98 A series of civil wars takes place in France.

1568-1648 Dutch War of Independence against Spain.

1572 Massacre of Huguenots on St. Bartholomew's Eve.

1588 England's navy defeats the Spanish Armada.

1598 Henry IV of France grants tolerance to the Huguenots in the Edict of Nantes.

1618-48 The Thirty Years' War ravages Germany.

1685 Toleration for Huguenots in France is ended by Louis XIV.

THE WORST WAR

The Thirty Years' War was the most vicious religious war of the time. It began in 1618 when Bohemia, which was part of the Holy Roman Empire, chose a Protestant king instead of one from the Catholic Hapsburg family. War broke out with Catholic Spain and Austria on one side and German Protestants, supported by Denmark, Sweden and later France, on the other side.

The French were Catholic, but they backed the Protestants because the Hapsburgs were their enemies. For thirty years, foreign armies ravaged Germany. The population fell dramatically as people were driven away or killed. The war ended in 1648 with the Treaty of Westphalia, which greatly reduced the Hapsburg Emperor's control over the German princes.

FIND OUT MORE

Catholicism ◄ 30

Charles V ◄ 37

See above pages for more information.

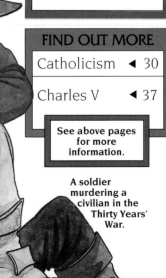

A soldier murdering a civilian in the Thirty Years' War.

POWER IN EUROPE

During the 16th century, many bitter wars had been caused by differences in religious belief. Now in the 17th century, countries waged wars to increase their territory, for power and glory and to win trade.

An English Civil War helmet.

KING AND PARLIAMENT

In the early 17th century, a theory, called the Divine Right of Kings, stated that kings and queens were appointed by God and were answerable only to Him. Like other monarchs, Charles I of England believed in this and thought that no one should criticize him or take over his powers. However, some members of the English Parliament began to demand a greater say in government.

A Civil War pikeman in Cromwell's New Model Army. The soldiers all wore red coats.

This clash of ideas led to the Civil War. Thanks to the leadership of Oliver Cromwell and his efficient "New Model Army", Parliament won and Charles was beheaded. Cromwell took the title Lord Protector and set up a republic.

The English people, though, began to dislike the new regime. On Cromwell's death, they invited Charles's son to become Charles II. From then on, the power of Parliament increased.

THE CIVIL WAR

This map shows which areas mainly supported Parliament and which supported the King, at the outbreak of the Civil War in 1642.

KEY

✕ Battle sites

Under control of Parliament

Under control of the King

SCOTLAND

In 1642, many Scots supported Parliament.

Edinburgh • ✕ Dunbar

In 1651, the Scots helped Charles II to invade England but were defeated.

IRELAND

Drogheda ✕

Dublin •

Uprisings in Ireland in support of the King were savagely stopped by Cromwell.

Wexford ✕

Irish Sea

Adwalton Moor ✕ ✕ Marston Moor
✕ Preston

ENGLAND

✕ Naseby

Worcester ✕   Edgehill ✕

WALES   Oxford •

Roundway Down ✕   ✕ Newbury   London •

Langport ✕

✕ Lostwithiel

| 0 | 100 | 200 km |
| 0 | | 100 miles |

N
W   E
S

THE RISE OF THE GERMAN PRINCES

At this time, there were more than 300 separate states in Germany. Some were ruled by princes and others by Catholic bishops. All the states formed the Holy Roman Empire, but the Emperor had little real control.

After the Thirty Years' War, many princes controlled their own states. Some became much stronger, especially Prussia. Its ruler was crowned King of Prussia in 1701 and it became a European power.

SWEDEN
BALTIC SEA
DENMARK
EAST PRUSSIA
BRANDENBURG
HOLY ROMAN EMPIRE

In 1618, the rulers of Brandenburg, the Hohenzollern family, took over Prussia.

SWEDEN
BALTIC SEA
DENMARK
EAST POMERANIA
EAST PRUSSIA
BRANDENBURG
HOLY ROMAN EMPIRE

At the end of the Thirty Years' War in 1648, Brandenburg-Prussia gained more land by the Treaty of Westphalia.

SWEDEN
BALTIC SEA
DENMARK
POMERANIA
PRUSSIA
HOLY ROMAN EMPIRE

By 1740, Brandenburg-Prussia, now known as Prussia, was an important state. It dominated Germany in the 18th century.

Prussian Giant Grenadiers. To be a "Giant Grenadier", men had to be enormously tall.

THE SUN KING

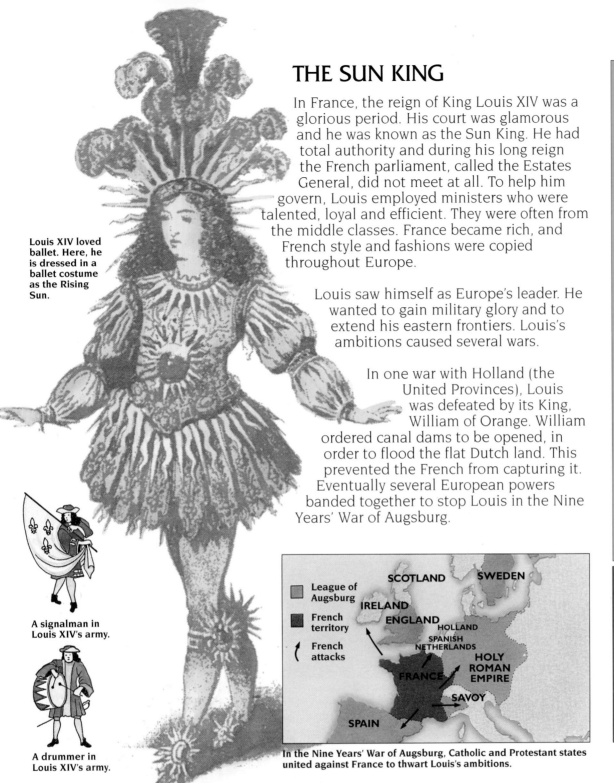

Louis XIV loved ballet. Here, he is dressed in a ballet costume as the Rising Sun.

A signalman in Louis XIV's army.

A drummer in Louis XIV's army.

In France, the reign of King Louis XIV was a glorious period. His court was glamorous and he was known as the Sun King. He had total authority and during his long reign the French parliament, called the Estates General, did not meet at all. To help him govern, Louis employed ministers who were talented, loyal and efficient. They were often from the middle classes. France became rich, and French style and fashions were copied throughout Europe.

Louis saw himself as Europe's leader. He wanted to gain military glory and to extend his eastern frontiers. Louis's ambitions caused several wars.

In one war with Holland (the United Provinces), Louis was defeated by its King, William of Orange. William ordered canal dams to be opened, in order to flood the flat Dutch land. This prevented the French from capturing it. Eventually several European powers banded together to stop Louis in the Nine Years' War of Augsburg.

League of Augsburg
French territory
French attacks

SCOTLAND SWEDEN
IRELAND
ENGLAND
HOLLAND
SPANISH NETHERLANDS
FRANCE
HOLY ROMAN EMPIRE
SAVOY
SPAIN

In the Nine Years' War of Augsburg, Catholic and Protestant states united against France to thwart Louis's ambitions.

WAR OF THE SPANISH SUCCESSION

In 1701, the sickly Charles II of Spain died. He had no son or brothers, but there were several candidates for the throne. Even though Louis XIV's Spanish wife had given up her right to the Spanish throne, Louis claimed it for his grandson, Philip of Anjou.

Other European nations declared war, forming a Grand Alliance against France. Eventually France was exhausted and a treaty was drawn up, called the Peace of Utrecht. Philip of Anjou became King of Spain, but the Spanish Empire was broken up.

GREAT BRITAIN
HOLY ROMAN EMPIRE
FRANCE
SPAIN
Gibraltar
Minorca

After the Peace of Utrecht, Britain gained Gibraltar and Minorca from Spain.

United Austrian Netherlands (formerly the Spanish Netherlands)
FRANCE
AUSTRIA
Milan
Naples
Sardinia

Austria won the Spanish Netherlands, plus Milan, Sardinia and Naples from France.

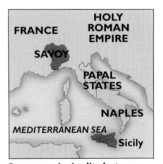

FRANCE
HOLY ROMAN EMPIRE
SAVOY
PAPAL STATES
NAPLES
MEDITERRANEAN SEA
Sicily

Savoy, a principality between France and Italy, gained the island of Sicily from Spain.

A 17th century naval battle. England, France, Spain and Holland all had strong navies.

THE RUSSIAN EMPIRE

Ivan III, the Great – Tsar of Russia from 1462-1505.

Ivan IV, the Terrible – Tsar from 1533-84.

In the 14th century, much of Russia was ruled by a group of Mongols called the Tartars. The Russian princes were forced to pay a tribute to the Tartars so that they would not attack Russia. Soon, though, a new Russian Empire was to emerge under the leadership of the Moscow princes.

RUSSIAN INDEPENDENCE

In 1328, the Tartars gave the ruler of Moscow, Ivan I, the job of collecting the tribute from the other Russian princes. This earned him the title "Moneybags". Moscow's importance now began to grow. Then, during the rule of Ivan III, the Great, the city itself began to grow. He married a Byzantine princess from Constantinople and declared that Moscow was to be the third Rome (after Rome itself and Constantinople). He then conquered the territory of Novgorod and refused to pay his tribute to the Tartars. Russia was now at last independent.

Moscow territory in 1389. From 1300 to the second half of the century, the Moscow princes expanded their territory. In 1380, they won a spectacular victory over the Tartars at the Battle of Kulikovo.

Moscow territory in 1462 at the start of Ivan the Great's reign. By this time, it had expanded again. In 1480, Ivan stopped paying the Tartars their tribute and now Russia was fully independent.

Moscow territory in 1505 at the end of Ivan the Great's reign. Ivan conquered Novgorod in 1478 and extended his control in all other directions. In 1500, he began attacking and taking territory from Lithuania.

IVAN IV

Ivan IV's crown, made in the Byzantine style.

The Russian emblem – the double-headed eagle.

Russia continued to expand during the reign of Ivan IV, the Terrible. He came to the throne in 1533 at age three and grew into a ruthless, clever man. He reformed the government to make himself absolute ruler. He also ordered the conquest of Siberia – the great area of forest and frozen land stretching to the east.

Ivan also issued a law which took rights away from peasants. They became serfs – people who could not leave their master's land. Ivan destroyed everyone who opposed him.

St. Basil's Cathedral in Moscow, built by Ivan the Terrible in 1552.

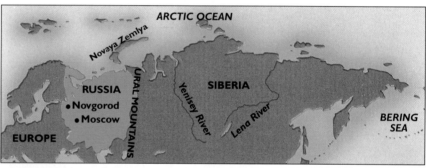

Russian territory in 1581. It was in this year that Ivan the Terrible ordered the exploration of Siberia to the east.

Russian territory in 1618. The Russians had now advanced from the Ural Mountains as far as the Yenisey River.

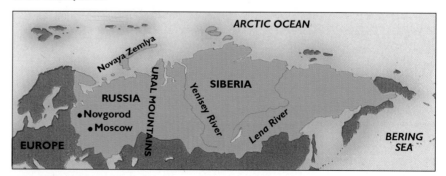

Russian territory in 1689. By the start of Peter the Great's reign in this year, Russia had expanded across Siberia.

A 16th century Cossack horseman.

Cossacks wore no breastplates or chainmail. They preferred to wear clothes that gave them freedom of movement.

Cossacks fought on horseback. They acted as mercenaries – soldiers who fought for money.

THE RUSSIAN PEOPLE

From early in its history, all the land in Russia was owned by noble families. Between the 10th and the 12th centuries, a group of noblemen emerged called the Boyars. These were important men who owned very large estates. They had a great deal of independence, and this often brought them into conflict with the Tsars.

Russian peasants were tied to the land and had to work for their local lord. In return, their lord gave them a certain amount of protection, but their lives were very hard.

One group of Russians who were independent from the noblemen were the Cossacks. The Cossacks lived in military communities on the frontiers of Russia, around the rivers Don and Dnieper. They were splendid horsemen and the Moscow princes used them to protect their frontiers against invaders such as the Tartars, Turks and Poles.

In later years, the Tsars of Russia used the Cossacks to help them explore and colonize Siberia.

TIME CHART

1328 Head of local Orthodox Church moves to Moscow.

1328-40 Ivan I, nicknamed Moneybags, rules Moscow.

1380 Moscow princes win victory over Tartars at Kulikovo.

1462-1505 Reign of Ivan III, the Great.

1478 Ivan the Great conquers Novgorod.

1480 Ivan refuses to pay tribute to Tartars.

1533-84 Reign of Ivan IV, the Terrible.

1558-82 Russia and Poland are at war.

1581 Ivan the Terrible orders first explorations of Siberia.

1613-45 Reign of Michael Romanov – the first of the Romanov Tsars.

1689-1725 Reign of Peter the Great.

1700-1721 The Great Northern War.

1703 Peter the Great founds St. Petersburg.

1721 Treaty of Nystadt gives Baltic States and part of Finland to Russia.

PETER THE GREAT

In 1689, Peter the Great became Tsar (or Emperor) at age 17. He was determined to modernize Russia and began a system of reforms. Although these reforms had an enormous effect, many were unpopular.

In order to learn as much as possible, Peter went to Europe, training in navigation and shipbuilding. He brought foreign craftsmen to modernize Russia, and built ports and canals. He also founded a new capital, St. Petersburg, on the Baltic coast. To do this, he had to advance into Swedish territory.

The Winter Palace in St. Petersburg, built by Peter's daughter Elizabeth.

THE GREAT NORTHERN WAR

Peter's expansion led to a war with Sweden's King Charles XII. This war, called The Great Northern War, began in 1700.

Although the Swedes started well, in 1709 they were heavily defeated at Poltava. Their army was eventually forced to flee to the Ottoman Empire. Russia then invaded Sweden itself in 1719. In 1721 the war ended with a treaty called the Peace of Nystadt. Peter the Great kept his newly acquired territory in the Baltic.

SWEDEN RUSSIA
Moscow •
Warsaw
Poltava
POLAND
➔ Charles's advance
✕ Battle

Charles XII of Sweden advanced into Russia in 1709. He was defeated at the Battle of Poltava.

SWEDEN
BALTIC SEA
St. Petersburg
RUSSIA
■ Sweden
□ Peter's conquests
□ Russia

As a result of the war, Peter gained more territory around the Baltic from Sweden.

FIND OUT MORE

Byzantine Empire	◀ 30
Mongols	◀ 34
Russia	▶ 62

See above pages for more information.

CHINA – THE MIDDLE KINGDOM

For many centuries, China enjoyed a brilliant and highly developed culture, although at times it was politically very unstable. For much of this time, the Chinese had little or nothing at all to do with foreigners, believing that there was nothing that they could gain from them. They called their land the Middle Kingdom.

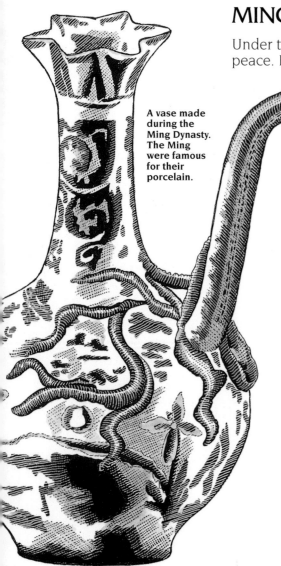

One of the marble statues which guards the entrance to the tombs of the Ming Emperors.

A Chinese printing block and inks. The Chinese invented printing.

THE MING DYNASTY

In 1368, a Buddhist monk called Chu Yuan-chang led a revolt in China against the Mongols, who ruled in China at that time. His revolt succeeded and Chu Yuan-chang founded a new family of Chinese rulers called the Ming Dynasty.

The early Ming rulers extended the Great Wall of China, which had originally been built to keep the Mongols out. They also brought the province of Yunnan under their control and forced Korea to pay a tribute to China. Soon, though, the Chinese decided to withdraw from foreign contacts altogether. They were self-sufficient and did not want anything from abroad. They regarded foreigners as barbarians – uncivilized people.

The Ming Empire in the 15th century. The Ming took control over the whole of China, including the southwest, which was not traditionally part of China.

MING CULTURE

Under the Ming Dynasty, China enjoyed 150 years of peace. During this time, the Chinese made many discoveries in medicine and craftsmen produced wonderful porcelain. They planted beautiful gardens and the Ming emperors were buried in magnificent tombs, guarded by huge statues. They were also great explorers. The most famous explorer was Admiral Cheng Ho, who made seven great voyages.

A vase made during the Ming Dynasty. The Ming were famous for their porcelain.

Eventually the state started to fall apart. There were many rebellions and one million people died in one rebellion alone. Bandits occupied the capital Peking (Beijing) and the Ming government collapsed.

The voyages of Admiral Cheng Ho between 1405 and 1433. Among other places, he sailed to Indochina, Indonesia, the Persian Gulf, Arabia and the east coast of Africa.

THE MANCHU DYNASTY

To the northeast of China lay the province of Manchuria, which was dependent on China for protection. Its people were nomads but around the year 1600, the tribes united. In the mid 1640s, the Chinese invited Manchu warriors into China to help them deal with the bandits. The Manchus soon established themselves as the new rulers, in control of the army.

Marriage between Chinese and Manchus was forbidden and they lived in separate areas of the cities. Chinese men had to wear their hair in pigtails to identify them.

Manchuria, the Manchus' homeland, northeast of China itself. Until around 1600, the Manchus were tribes of nomads. They went on to conquer China.

THE EMPIRE EXPANDS

The Manchu Empire grew as China prospered. Taiwan, Mongolia, Tibet and Turkestan all came under its rule. Trade increased, especially in tea, and the Chinese style became very fashionable in 18th century Europe.

By the late 18th century, however, dislike of foreigners was steadily growing again. The Chinese prevented Christian missionaries from preaching in China. Attempts by Europeans to increase trade were soundly snubbed.

When the British diplomat Lord McCartney visited Peking on a trading mission in 1793, he was told very firmly by Chinese officials that there was nothing at all that China needed to buy from barbarians like him.

An 18th century European ornament, made in the Chinese style. Europeans copied Chinese art styles in furniture, ornaments and wall hangings.

18th century Chinese style wallpaper pattern.

The Manchu Empire at its greatest extent around the year 1760. Korea had at one time been under China's protection but was by now independent.

THE OPIUM WARS

In the 19th century, Europeans were anxious to buy tea from China, but the Chinese did not want European goods. Europeans had to pay for tea in silver. There was one thing, however, that the Chinese merchants did want – a drug from India called opium.

At this time, the British ruled India and supplied opium to China although it was banned there. The Chinese government was very angry about this and two wars broke out between Britain and China. China was defeated twice. As a result of the wars, called the Opium Wars, Hong Kong plus five other ports were given to Britain for trading purposes. Other European nations were also able to use trading ports. The Manchus were humiliated by this and the Europeans' influence weakened their rule.

The six British Treaty Ports of 1842. Other European nations also had influence over different areas of China, which they used for trade purposes.

THE BOXER REBELLION

In the late 19th century, China was dominated by a very powerful woman called Tz'u-hsi. When the Emperor died in 1862, her baby, the Emperor's only son, came to the throne. She ruled for him and then held on to power when he died. She was determined not to accept any change in China.

In 1899 a secret society, known as the Boxers, rebelled against foreigners in Peking. Christians were attacked and for nearly two months, foreign embassies were put under siege, supported by Tz'u-hsi. Concern in Europe led to an international force being sent to rescue the foreign traders. They defeated the Boxers and from then on foreigners were able to enter China much more freely.

Tz'u-hsi, the Dowager Empress who ruled China from 1862-1908.

49

THE SLAVE TRADE

Slavery had been part of life since very early times. Between the 17th to the 19th centuries a massive trade existed between Africa and the Americas, as millions of Africans were sent to work in the New World.

A slave driver, whose job it was to make slaves work hard.

A female slave who may have worked on a plantation.

THE AFRICAN SLAVE TRADE BEGINS

$1200 TO 1250 DOLLARS! FOR NEGROES!!

THE undersigned wishes to purchase a large lot of NEGROES for the New Orleans market. I will pay $1200 to $1250 for No. 1 young men, and $850 to $1000 for No. 1 young women. In fact I will pay more for likely

NEGROES,

Than any other trader in Kentucky. My office is adjoining the Broadway Hotel, on Broadway, Lexington, Ky., where I or my Agent can always be found.

WM. F. TALBOTT.

LEXINGTON, JULY 2, 1853.

This American poster of 1853 offers up to $1,250 for a group of African slaves. The slave trade was a big business.

When Europeans began to arrive in the Americas, they opened mines and large farms, called plantations, for producing goods to send back to Europe. The Europeans forced the native Americans to work for them, but many died due to the harsh working conditions and European diseases.

As a result, the plantations and mines were short of workers. To solve this problem, a regular trade was set up to transport Africans to the Americas so that they could work for the Europeans there. Over past centuries, Mediterranean people had used Africans as slaves. However, this new slave trade was bigger than any earlier ones.

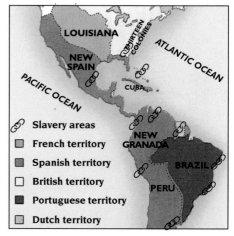

Key:
- Slavery areas
- French territory
- Spanish territory
- British territory
- Portuguese territory
- Dutch territory

European colonies in the Americas, where African slaves worked.

SLAVE TRIANGLE

In the mid-18th century, at the peak of the trade, slave ships left Europe with guns, cloth and goods, such as beads and mirrors. These were produced cheaply in Europe.

The ships sailed to West Africa or Madagascar, where the goods were sold to local chiefs in exchange for slaves. Some were criminals or prisoners of war, but others were simply kidnapped from their villages and sold.

A slave fort on the West African coast, where captured slaves were taken.

THE SLAVE TRIANGLE

This map shows the triangular trade and the goods exchanged between the three continents. A separate slave trade in East Africa supplied the Arab world.

1. From Europe, ships sailed to Africa with fancy goods, such as cloth and trinkets.

3. In the Americas, slaves were sold for cash or exchanged for metals and foodstuffs.

2. In Africa, captains packed their ships with slaves.

KEY
- Coffee
- Cotton
- Rice
- Sugar
- Tobacco
- Slave origin

0   5000 km

0   3000 miles

THE SLAVES' FATE

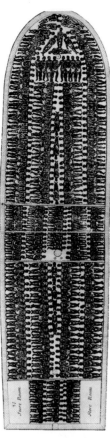

A diagram of a slave ship, showing how people were packed in tightly together.

Most African slaves landed in South America or the Caribbean and the rest went to North America. In the early years, as many as a quarter of the slaves died during the two month voyage. Conditions were cramped, unhealthy and hot, and the people were chained.

In later years, some captains gave slaves exercise, washed out their quarters and gave them better food and care. They did this to keep more slaves alive in order to make more money.

Slaves who survived the voyage were sold at auctions. If they were lucky, they might be bought by someone who would treat them kindly. Most, though, were forced to work hard in the fields. In all, it is thought that between 10 and 12 million Africans were enslaved like this.

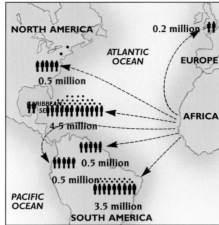

African slaves were sent mainly to the Caribbean islands, but also to Europe, North America and South America.

A slave branding iron. Slaves were burned, or branded, with a hot iron like this one, showing their new owner's initials.

REBELLIONS AND ESCAPES

Toussaint L'Ouverture was made Governor-General of Haiti for life, but was later betrayed and died in a French prison.

Some slaves rebelled. Most rebellions were stopped savagely, but one succeeded brilliantly. In 1804, the slaves of Haiti, led by Toussaint L'Ouverture, fought the French and won Haiti's freedom.

Other slaves ran away. In North America, there was an organized escape route to Canada, where slaves would be free, nicknamed the Underground Railroad. One of the bravest to help escapers was an ex-slave named Harriet Tubman. In all, she helped 19 groups of people to freedom.

The United States of America. Slavery was legal in the southern states.

THE ANTI-SLAVERY CAMPAIGN

In 1807, a politician called William Wilberforce persuaded the British government to pass a law which banned British ships from taking part in slavery. In 1823, he helped to found the Anti-Slavery Society, which tried to abolish slavery in the British Empire. In 1833, this happened at last.

In 1808 a law was passed banning the import of slaves to the United States. However, it was still legal for people to own slaves. In the northern states, many people wanted slavery abolished, but people in southern states relied upon slaves to work. This difference in opinion was one of the causes of the American Civil War.

The Wedgwood Medallion – a popular symbol of the Anti-Slavery Society.

TIME CHART

c.1450 African slaves begin to be taken to Europe.

c.1520 African slaves begin to be taken to America by Europeans.

1522 The first slave rebellion takes place in Hispaniola.

c.1750 The slave trade is at its peak.

1772 Slavery is declared illegal in England.

1792 Slavery is banned in Danish colonies.

1794 Slavery is banned in French colonies.

1804 A slave rebellion succeeds in Haiti.

1807 Wilberforce's law bans British ships from taking part in slavery.

1808 The US government bans slaves from being brought into the country.

1822 The USA founds Liberia in Africa as a colony for freed slaves.

c.1830 Spanish colonies gain independence and slavery starts to die out.

1833 Slavery is abolished in the British Empire.

c.1850-61 The Underground Railroad in North America helps slaves to freedom.

1861-65 The American Civil War. The northern states are victorious.

1863 Lincoln declares all slaves in the United States of America free.

1888 Slavery is abolished in Brazil.

FIND OUT MORE

American Civil War	▶	61
Africa	◀	25
New World	◀	40

See above pages for more information.

THE RISE OF JAPAN

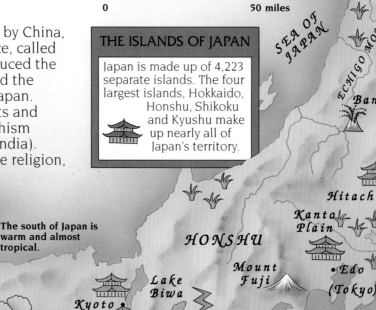

Japan is a chain of mountainous islands off the eastern coast of Asia. The Japanese are an ancient people, who developed their own traditions and religion over the centuries. Though Japan's culture was greatly influenced by China, until the 19th century it had little contact with the rest of the world.

The Temple of the Golden Pavilion near Kyoto, built in the 14th century.

JAPAN IN ANCIENT TIMES

Japan was, and still is, a place with many natural hazards. The islands are very prone to earthquakes, which can be followed by terrible fires and tsunami – giant waves in the sea caused by earthquakes. Nevertheless, people kept migrating to the islands from southeast Asia over a very long period of time. As more and more people arrived, they began to dominate Japan's original inhabitants, who were called the Ainu. The Ainu came to hold a very low position in Japanese society after their defeat in their great uprising in 812AD.

JAPANESE CULTURE

Japan became heavily influenced by China, mostly due to a 7th century prince, called Prince Shotuku. In 604, he introduced the Chinese calendar, civil service and the Chinese style of government to Japan. He also brought in Chinese artists and craftsmen and encouraged Buddhism (which had come to China from India). However, Shintoism, the Japanese religion, remained strong.

JAPAN

Nowadays, the Ainu people live in areas created specially for them in Hokkaido.

Northern Honshu has always been a major rice growing area.

The climate of north Japan is cool, like the European climate.

HOKKAIDO

Tarumae

Usu

0 ___ 50 km

0 ___ 50 miles

THE ISLANDS OF JAPAN

Japan is made up of 4,223 separate islands. The four largest islands, Hokkaido, Honshu, Shikoku and Kyushu make up nearly all of Japan's territory.

SEA OF JAPAN

ECHIGO MOUNTAINS

Bandai

KEY

	Volcano
	Major earthquake zone
	Major city
	Rice growing
	Coniferous forest
	Deciduous and sub-tropical forest

Hitachi

Kanto Plain

HONSHU

Mount Fuji

Edo (Tokyo)

The south of Japan is warm and almost tropical.

Lake Biwa

Kyoto

Osaka Sakai

Kanakura

PACIFIC OCEAN

N / W / E / S

Hiroshima

SHIKOKU

Kii Peninsula

Mount Unzen

Nagasaki

KYUSHU

Sakurajima

A 17th century shogun, drawn in the Japanese style.

EMPERORS AND SHOGUNS

According to legend, the first Emperor was Jimmu Tenno, who came to the throne around 660BC. The Japanese believed that emperors were gods and that they were all-powerful.

In the 9th century, a family called Fujiwara gained control over the court. Other families challenged them, causing years of feuding. In 1192, Minamoto Yoritomo won and took the title Shogun. This was a military title, but the holder ran the government too. From then on, the Emperor had little power, although he was still a god to his people.

THE MONGOL INVASIONS

Due to Japan's strong island position, it was very safe from invasions by other nations. However in both 1274 and 1281, the Mongol rulers of China attempted to invade Japan. On both occasions, the Mongols failed when they were forced back by violent winds that wrecked and scattered the Mongol fleet. In Japan, these winds are known as *kamikaze* or "divine winds".

SAMURAI WARRIORS

By the 12th century, a group of warriors, called the samurai, had emerged during Japan's many wars. The samurai were highly skilled and had a strict code of conduct.

From 1339 to 1573, called the Ashikaga Period, the shoguns gradually lost control over the landowners, who were known as the daimyos. The daimyos were very powerful and continually fought each other. They employed huge armies of samurai and built massive castles. By the 16th century, the title of samurai was handed down from father to son. Only samurai were allowed to carry weapons.

After the Ashikaga Period, rival leaders fought for control of Japan. Following a great victory at the battle of Sekigahara in 1600, an important daimyo called Tokugawa Ieyasu became Shogun. He limited the powers of the other daimyos and his descendants kept the title until 1868. Japan was peaceful and prosperous under their reign.

TRADE WITH JAPAN

The Japanese were suspicious of foreigners and in 1639, all foreign traders were banned, except for a few Dutch and Chinese, who were only allowed to trade in Nagasaki.

However, in 1853, an American officer, called Commodore Perry, arrived in Japan on a trade mission. By this time, Japan was facing economic problems and Perry was able to force Japan to allow Europeans and Americans to trade there.

JAPAN MODERNIZES

The arrival of foreigners caused a lot of confusion in Japan. In 1868, the emperor took advantage of this and grabbed power back for himself in a surprise move. He then began to modernize the country and took control of the government.

Tokyo became the capital and the Japanese quickly adopted western science and technology. As a result of this modernization effort, Japan soon became the dominant power in Asia.

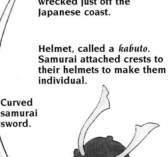

The Mongol fleets were wrecked just off the Japanese coast.

Helmet, called a *kabuto*. Samurai attached crests to their helmets to make them individual.

Curved samurai sword.

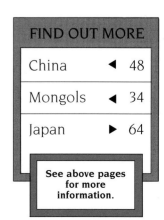

Samurai warriors wore protective plates made from iron, leather and fabric over the chest, back, arms and legs.

A samurai warrior of the 16th century in traditional costume.

In 1894, Japanese troops landed in Korea, which was a separate state, but protected by China. They then advanced further north into Manuchuria.

China lost the war in 1895. It was forced to give Korea independence and hand over Taiwan and the Kwangtung Peninsula to Japan.

INDUSTRIAL REVOLUTION

The first iron bridge was built in Shropshire, England in 1779.

During the 18th and 19th centuries, Britain was transformed from a nation of farmers to an industrial giant – "the workshop of the world". From Britain, the Industrial Revolution spread across Europe and the world.

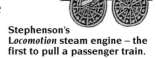

Stephenson's *Locomotion* steam engine – the first to pull a passenger train.

AGRICULTURAL CHANGE

In 1700, much of Britain was still farmed in medieval-style open fields. But in the 18th century, scientific developments helped farmers to improve their soil with natural and chemical fertilizers. The late 18th century saw improvements too in breeding farm animals. Farmers produced plenty of food to keep pace with the growing population.

To profit from the new farming methods rich landowners ended the open field system and did away with the common land. They enclosed their land into large private farms, ignoring opposition from small landowners.

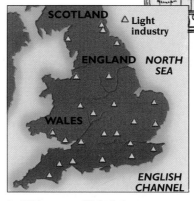

This picture shows a homeless farmer and his family. Many small farmers could not survive in the new system. Some found work on rich landowners' farms. Many went to the cities to work in factories.

STEAM POWER

Late in the 17th century, James Watt first patented the steam engine. At first many industrialists were wary, but soon they saw that steam could free them from the seasonal changes of water power. Factories could also be built at more convenient places. Steam soon overtook water as a key energy source.

By the late 18th century, steam-driven machinery was powering mine shaft pumps, iron foundries, cotton mills. Later, it also powered the trains and ships which carried all the new manufactured goods.

THE INDUSTRIAL REVOLUTION

The 18th and 19th centuries in Britain saw dramatic changes in the way people worked and where they lived. Manufacturing shifted rapidly from small cottage industries to huge mills and factories. Towns and cities grew up around factories to house the workers.

New machines were invented to do the jobs of spinners, weavers and other skilled workers. Fewer people could now produce more goods. Some machines worked so simply that children could mind them – for much lower rates of pay.

Skilled workers now received vastly reduced wages, or were put out of work altogether. Many could no longer afford to feed their families. Whole families were forced to work longer and longer hours, often in dark, dirty and sometimes dangerous conditions.

Angry and violent protests broke out regularly over the early decades of the 19th century. One group, called the Luddites, protested against the situation by breaking up the new machinery responsible for taking their jobs. Revolts such as these were crushed harshly by the authorities.

SCOTLAND △ Light industry

ENGLAND NORTH SEA

WALES

ENGLISH CHANNEL

In 1700, areas of light industry were scattered all over Britain. At this time, three quarters of the population worked on the land.

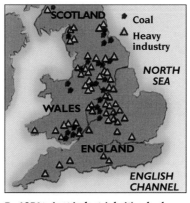

SCOTLAND ● Coal △ Heavy industry

NORTH SEA

WALES

ENGLAND

ENGLISH CHANNEL

By 1851, giant industrial cities had sprung up around the mills, factories and coalfields. Millions came to the cities to find work.

CLOTH

New inventions like the Flying Shuttle and the Spinning Jenny, produced woven cloth far more quickly and cheaply than by hand.

As the technology developed, larger and larger machines were driven by huge water wheels and then by steam power. Great mills were built deep in river valleys to house the power looms. Crowded towns and cities grew up quickly alongside so that the thousands of factory workers could live nearby. Children worked the same long hours as adults, and orphans and homeless children were often apprenticed as cheap workers.

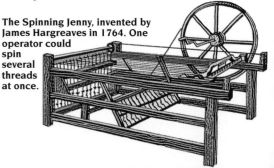

The Spinning Jenny, invented by James Hargreaves in 1764. One operator could spin several threads at once.

TIME CHART

1733 Kay invents the Flying Shuttle weaving machine.

1761 The Bridgewater Canal opens.

1782 James Watt patents his rotary steam engine.

1811-12 Luddite rebels break industrial machinery.

1812 The first gas light company established in London.

1825 The first passenger railway service opens between Stockton and Darlington in northeast England.

1851 The Great Exhibition displays to the world Britain's technological achievements.

1870s Regular crossings of the Atlantic, and other long distance routes by steam ship, begin.

1871 Trade unions become legal in Britain.

1876 Alexander Graham Bell invents the telephone, in the USA.

1885 First internal combustion engine is invented in Germany.

FIND OUT MORE

Trade unions ▶58

19th century ▶62

See above pages for more information.

COAL, IRON AND STEEL

In 1709 Abraham Darby discovered a new, cheap way to use coal to smelt top-quality iron. Iron foundries sprang up near the coalfields. "King Coal", as it was called, powered the new iron age, with a bewildering variety of iron goods from knives and forks to machines, bridges and steam ships. Cheap steel came much later.

The miners' safety lamp reduced the risk of explosions.

The iron and steel industries flourished making weapons for the many wars of the age.

Steam trains brought fresh food into the cities, and up-to-date news and goods to the remote countryside.

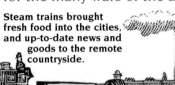

Metal goods, like scissors, became a major export.

TRANSPORT

Until the mid-18th century in Britain, horse-drawn travel on poor roads was slow and expensive. In 1761 the first canal halved the cost of carrying coal into Manchester.

George Stephenson opened the first passenger steam railway in the world in 1825, and "Railway Mania" set in soon afterwards.

Within 35 years over 16,000km (10,000 miles) of track were built, carrying nearly 80 million passengers each year. Freight trains transported manufactured goods across the nation.

The first railways, built by 1840.

Railways built by 1850, just ten years later.

Railways by 1880. A vast new network of railway lines now covered much of Europe.

EFFECTS OF THE REVOLUTION

By the 1870s, Britain was responsible for producing one third of the world's industrial output. Some people became fantastically rich from the profits. But for many more people, the changes brought misery. The new cities were overcrowded, dirty and full of disease. Men, women and children worked up to 16 hours a day for low wages and in dangerous conditions.

Workers who tried to form trade unions to protect their rights were severely punished. Unions had become legal only in 1871. Slowly Parliament began to pass laws to force employers to improve conditions in factories. New laws also made sure all children went to school, and improved public health and housing.

These young women, matchmakers at Bryant and May, won safer working conditions after a strike in 1888.

THE SPREAD OF THE REVOLUTION

Soon other European nations, led by Belgium, Germany, France and Switzerland, as well as the United States, began to challenge Britain's lead in industrialization. These other countries developed steel and electrical industries, in which Britain never achieved the same supremacy.

In the USA, the modern world began to take shape with inventions like the typewriter, telephone, the electric lamp bulb and the sewing machine. Germany pioneered the car industry with the internal combustion engine in 1885.

Alexander Graham Bell invented the telephone in 1876. It went on to revolutionize communications around the world.

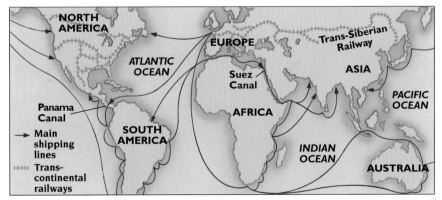

Iron steamships started to cross the Atlantic regularly from the 1870s. Railways and steamships carried manufactured goods around the world, transforming world trade and bringing industrial expansion to the United States of America, Canada, South America, Siberia (in Russia) and Australia.

THE AGE OF REVOLUTIONS

In Europe in the 18th century, new ideas began to spring up about government and the rights of all people. People became more self-confident, especially the prosperous middle classes. They began to believe in freedom of thought and became more tolerant of different religions. For this reason, this time was known as the Age of Reason or "The Enlightenment".

A French revolutionary.

Although badly armed and equipped, the revolutionaries succeeded by sheer numbers.

The guillotine – used to behead members of the nobility during the French Revolution.

The victim lay on the bench. His or her head was severed by a blade from above and dumped in the basket.

THE ENLIGHTENED DESPOTS

Many 18th century monarchs had absolute power. Some did not rule very well or care about their subjects. Other monarchs, called the Enlightened Despots, were different. They were still "despots" (in that they had absolute power), but they worked hard to improve their countries. Maria Theresa of Austria, Frederick the Great of Prussia and Catherine the Great of Russia were all Enlightened Despots.

THE FRENCH REVOLUTION

In 1789 a revolution broke out in France. It began simply as a movement which wanted to introduce a constitutional monarchy – one in which the king or queen is guided by a government elected by the people. Soon however, the lower classes were swept along with this movement, which became a full-scale revolution against the nobility. The king and queen were executed, along with many other nobles, during a period of a few months known as the Reign of Terror.

NAPOLEON'S EMPIRE

After the Revolution, France became dominated by Napoleon Bonaparte. In 1789 he was a poor, young officer but he rose to command the French army and then joined the government. He later took it over completely and made himself Emperor in 1804.

Napoleon Bonaparte

In a series of brilliant campaigns, Napoleon conquered most of Europe. He appeared to be unbeatable. Then, in 1805 the French navy was beaten at sea by the British under the command of Lord Nelson at the Battle of Trafalgar. From then on Britain ruled the seas, although the French army was still dominant on land.

THE FALL OF NAPOLEON

In 1812, Napoleon made a great mistake. He invaded Russia and advanced all the way to Moscow. The fleeing Russians burned Moscow and destroyed supplies. In the middle of the severe Russian winter, French troops had to retreat from the city, without enough provisions or equipment. Of the 610,000 men who invaded Russia, only 30,000 returned.

Prussia and Austria joined the fight with Britain against Napoleon, who was forced to abdicate in 1814. He was exiled to the island of Elba in the Mediterranean Sea. In 1815, however, he escaped to lead France once more, though he was finally beaten at the Battle of Waterloo. Napoleon was exiled again to the island of St. Helena, where he died in 1821. Following the collapse of the French Empire, the Congress of Vienna restored to the throne the monarchs who had been deposed by Napoleon.

The Battle of Trafalgar in 1805. It took place off the coasts of southern Spain and north Africa. The British were victorious.

The Peninsular War of 1808-14. Britain fought France in Spain and Portugal. The French army began to lose its dominance.

Under direct French control

Ruled by Napoleon's relatives

Satellite states

Europe in 1812 at the height of Napoleon's power in Europe. Some areas were controlled directly by his government in Paris. Some states were satellites of France – that is they were heavily influenced by it. Others were ruled by members of Napoleon's family.

Napoleon's invasion of Russia in 1812. The French army reached Moscow but had to retreat when the Russians set it on fire.

INDEPENDENCE FOR SOUTH AMERICA

In the 18th century, South America was still in the hands of Spain and Portugal who had set up colonies there in the 16th century.

Now, the revolutionary spirit which had swept Europe was affecting the people in South and Central America too. They began to want independence. Little by little, each country in South and Central America gained independence. An unhappy time followed, though, with many civil wars and also conflicts between the newly created states.

1846-48 Mexico is at war with the USA.

Mexican border 1848 After the war with the USA, Mexico loses 40% of its territory.

UNITED STATES OF AMERICA

TEXAS

1836 Texas becomes independent from Mexico. It joins the USA in 1848.

CUBA

MEXICO

BRITISH HONDURAS

GUATEMALA HONDURAS
EL SALVADOR
NICARAGUA

1811 Venezuela becomes independent. Simon Bolivar becomes dictator in 1813.

1838 Guatemala, Honduras, El Salvador, Nicaragua and Costa Rica become independent. Panama remains part of Colombia until 1903.

COSTA RICA

PANAMA

VENEZUELA

BRITISH GUIANA
DUTCH GUIANA
FRENCH GUIANA

1830 New Granada gains independence. From 1861 it is called Colombia.

COLOMBIA

1830 Ecuador gains independence.

ECUADOR

BRAZIL

A NEW SOUTH AMERICA

This map shows central and South America in the mid 19th century. By this time, all nations had gained their independence from Spain and Portugal.

PERU

1821 Peru gains independence.

BOLIVIA

1822 Brazil gains independence.

1825 Bolivia gains independence.

1865 Paraguay is at war with Brazil, Argentina and Uraguay. 70% of its population dies or leaves.

PARAGUAY

BRAZIL

In 1822, Brazil gained independence from Portugal. It was the only nation to achieve independence without armed conflict. It just separated from Portugal and became an independent empire under King Pedro I. The empire lasted until 1889 when, having abolished slavery, Pedro II was deposed by plantation owners and a republic was set up.

MEXICO

In 1821, Mexico declared independence from Spain and became a republic two years later. Its leader, General Santa Ana, defeated a Spanish invasion in 1829. In 1855 Santa Ana was overthrown and Mexico came under control of a man called Benito Juarez.

Civil war followed from 1858-61. France, Britain and Spain became involved and in 1863, France made Prince Maximillian of Austria Emperor of Mexico. Maximillian, though, lost power once French troops were withdrawn and he was shot on the orders of Juarez.

1810 Paraguay declares independence.

1816 Argentina gains independence.

URUGUAY

1828 Uraguay gains independence.

CHILE

ARGENTINA

0   250   500 km

0   150   300 miles

FIND OUT MORE

See above pages for more information.

THE RIGHT TO VOTE

During the 19th century, there was a growing call in Europe for greater democracy – the right to vote (or the franchise). People demanded free elections to choose their governments. For others the priority was to unite and form their own nation.

Women throughout society called for the vote. This badge is from the Actresses' Franchise League in Britain.

This figure from a Polish pamphlet called for freedom from Russian domination.

REVOLTS AND REPRESSION

Monarchs and emperors with absolute power were reluctant to give it up. Some tried to divert their people by improving living conditions. But revolts erupted throughout this period against regimes which allowed little real change.

Many revolts were crushed fiercely. In response, some people turned to violence as a way of achieving their goals. In Russia, for instance, terrorists assassinated the Tsar in 1881. Only at the end of the 19th century did the right to vote become widespread for men in Europe.

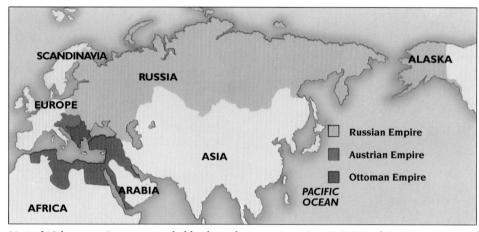

SCANDINAVIA RUSSIA ALASKA EUROPE ASIA ARABIA AFRICA PACIFIC OCEAN

☐ Russian Empire
■ Austrian Empire
■ Ottoman Empire

Most of 19th century Europe was ruled by these three great empires. Britain and France were wary of Russia's desire to expand, and tried to shore up the Ottoman Empire to keep the balance of power.

MOVEMENTS FOR CHANGE

Two new movements were developing in the 19th century. Workers' organizations, like the Chartists in 1840s Britain, paved the way for socialism and the international trade union movement. Socialism called for a just distribution of wealth, with equal rights and decent working conditions for all.

The aims of communism were also to achieve social justice, but by means of revolution. The state would take over running all factories and farms on behalf of the people. In 1848 the Communist Manifesto proclaimed "Workers of the world, unite!"

In 19th century Europe, nationalism became a great force. Nationalism is the feeling shared by people of one area that they are bound together by a common language, religion, culture and history. People wished to govern themselves, especially if they were under foreign rule. This posed a great threat to each empire.

This medal celebrates the elevation of the Prussian King to German Emperor in 1849 with the nationalist words, "For freedom, truth and German glory".

The British blacksmiths' union protected all members' rights. Its motto was "By hammer and hand all arts do stand".

REVOLTS IN FRANCE

After Napoleon's defeat in 1815, France was far from stable. The Bourbon King Louis XVIII had been restored to the throne but revolutions followed in 1830 and again in 1848, at the same time as nationalist rebellions right across Europe. A Prussian victory in 1870 caused the collapse of Napoleon III and the Second Empire. France faced a period of turmoil once more.

UNIFICATION OF ITALY

Italy consisted of several kingdoms and states under different rulers. A movement called *Il Risorgimento* called for unification – the joining together of separate states. In 1861 Giuseppe Garibaldi led his red-shirted volunteers in a revolt against the Austrian Empire. Italy was born.

In 1859 Italy was made up of many states. France supported her quest for unification.

By 1861 Italy was a single nation. Venetia and the Papal States joined by 1870.

POLAND AND HUNGARY

Poland revolted several times against its Russian rulers, who crushed the rebellions, and tried to stamp out Polish culture and nationalist feelings. In 1867 the Austrian Empire defeated Hungary's revolt too, but at least her people were still free to follow their own culture and language.

Strategically vital, Poland was the westernmost point of the Russian Empire.

Hungary did not achieve independence from Austria until after World War One.

THE BALKANS

The great Ottoman Empire was in decline. Christians in the Balkans wanted to break free, and Russia supported them, to undermine the Ottomans. In 1832 Greece achieved self-rule, but other regions like Serbia, Bosnia, Romania and Bulgaria had to wait until 1878 for indepedence.

Only Greece managed to break away from Ottoman rule early in the 19th century.

Many Balkan nations faced a long struggle for self rule. Conflict still dogs this region.

GERMANY

In 1815, Germany consisted of 39 states. The Prussian Chancellor, Bismarck, encouraged the nationalists' desire to join these states together. Already trade links were being fostered. Prussia won victories over Denmark, Austria and France. In 1871 William I became Kaiser of the united Germany.

Prussia dominated the many small states on its borders in central Europe after 1815.

By 1871, Germany was united. Her military power was to overshadow Europe.

TIME CHART

1815 Louis XVIII, the Bourbon king, is restored to the French throne after the Napoleonic Wars.

1830 Revolution in France. Louis Philippe of Orléans becomes King.

1830 Belgium becomes independent of Dutch rule.

1832 Greece becomes independent of Turkish Ottoman rule.

1832 Great Reform Act extends voting rights to more men in Britain.

1846-49 Rebellions in France, Poland, Germany, Italy and Hungary.

1861 Italy is unified. The Pope still rules the Vatican as an independent state.

1871 Germany achieves unification.

1881 Tsar Alexander II is assassinated.

1893 Women in New Zealand are the first to achieve the right to vote.

1906 First Labour members of Parliament elected in Britain.

1917 Russian Revolution.

FIND OUT MORE

Ottoman Empire	◄ 30
Russian Empire	◄ 46
Balkan crisis	► 65

See above pages for more information.

RUSSIAN REVOLUTION

One of the most dramatic revolutions against the state was in Russia. By 1917 the people were weary of their involvement in World War One. Sheer hunger led to strikes, and troops sent to quell the unrest mutinied instead. Tsar Nicholas abdicated.

The Bolshevik revolutionaries were led by Lenin, a follower of Karl Marx. They had wide support, promising peace, land and bread. In just five days in November 1917, they seized St. Petersburg and set up a communist government. The new regime had to grant independence to Poland, Finland and the Baltic states, but it crushed the nationalists in Armenia and Ukraine.

VOTES FOR WOMEN

Only late in the 19th century were women's calls for the vote considered. Even the French Revolution, with its cry "Liberty, Equality, Fraternity", excluded women from its demands.

New Zealand women were the first to achieve the vote in 1893, followed in 1907 by Norway and later by Denmark, Luxembourg and the Netherlands. In Britain and the USA, the Suffragette movement campaigned for women's right to vote. Their struggle was blocked until 1921. Then at last most women over the age of 30 were granted the right to vote, in return for women's work during the war.

Women organized protests and got themselves arrested to draw public attention to their cause.

THE BIRTH OF THE USA

By the start of the 18th century, many people were leaving Europe to settle in colonies in North America. The British, French and Spaniards all owned colonies in the east. Much territory was still occupied by the native North American Indians.

A fur trapper. Trappers were among the first Europeans to explore western North America.

An American Indian chief. Indians gradually lost their land to European settlers.

THE ROAD TO INDEPENDENCE

The British colonists on the east coast of North America were surrounded by French, Spanish and American Indian territories. Britain gradually gained more territory by treaties, as wars were fought both in America and in Europe. Although British victories helped their colonists gain wealth and territory, many of them began to want independence from Britain.

The colonists resented the fact that Britain controlled their trade. They also felt bitter because they had no say in the British parliament, yet they still had to pay taxes. The British government was not interested in exploring further west than the Appalachian Mountains. This disappointed the colonists, as many of them were eager to expand their territory.

Fur trappers were also known as "mountain men". They went west of the Appalachian mountains to make their fortunes.

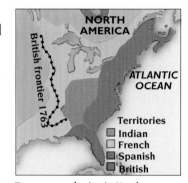

European colonies in North America by 1713. Britain had 13 colonies on the east coast of North America. By 1763 Britain was also in control of Canada, which it had won from France.

THE WAR OF INDEPENDENCE

George Washington (1732-99) became the first President of the United States. Here he is shown in his uniform as Colonel of the Virginia Militia.

The first armed clash between British troops and American colonists came at Lexington in April 1775. The War of Independence had now begun. In July 1776, the 13 colonies made their Declaration of Independence and became known as the United States.

The colonists, led by George Washington, lacked trained men, money and weapons. In contrast, the British army included mercenary soldiers and American Indians. The colonists, though, had an advantage, because they knew the countryside, which the British did not. The British also had problems with supplying men, arms and provisions, because they were so far from home. At last, the colonists were victorious and American independence was recognized at the Peace of Paris in 1783.

Battles between British troops and American colonists in the American War of Independence, 1775-83. All of the fighting took place in the former British colonies. The first battle was at Lexington.

THE USA GROWS

The United States soon began to grow. The population increased as more people arrived from Europe. People settled farther and farther west and these new territories were incorporated into the United States.

In 1803 Louisiana was bought from France and in 1819, Florida was bought from Spain. After a war with Mexico, the United States gained California, Texas and the Southwest Territories in 1848. Alaska was bought from Russia in 1867 and another war, this time with Spain, led to the United States gaining the islands of Puerto Rico and Guam in 1898. Hawaii also came under US control.

The United States of America in 1867. By this time it had acquired more territory – Louisiana from France, Texas from Mexico, Florida from Spain and Alaska from Russia. Canada was British.

THE GOLD RUSH

At first, only trappers, hunters and explorers ventured west of the Mississippi. Then in 1848 gold was discovered in California, and a manic hunt for gold began.

Gold miners set out to travel over 3,000km (2,000 miles) of wilderness. They faced great danger with lack of food and water, deserts, mountains and attacks by Indians. The gold rush soon died down, but farmers and their families now came in search of land.

Settlers journeyed west in covered wagons, like this one.

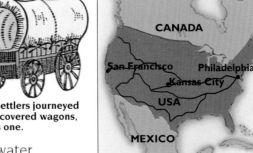

Trails leading west to new territories. Thousands followed these trails throughout the 19th century in search of land on which to settle and farm.

THE VANISHING INDIANS

The native American Indians of the great grassy areas of the West, known as the Great Plains, depended on hunting buffalo for their livelihood. As the settlers spread across the West, they killed off the buffalo and began to fence off the Indians' land. Not surprisingly the Indians fought to keep their land, but the settlers were protected by the US Army.

The Indians were few and poorly armed compared with the US Army and in the long run they could not win the war for their homeland. Many died in battles with the army and also of hunger and disease. Survivors were made to live in enclosed areas, called reservations. The last Indian battle was fought at Wounded Knee in South Dakota in 1890.

The Battle of Wounded Knee in 1890. This was the last battle between US forces and the Indians. Many Indians were killed, including women and children.

THE CIVIL WAR

In the mid-19th century, tension arose between the states of the North and the South. One of the many issues that divided them was slavery, which the North disagreed with but which the South relied upon. The South decided to leave the Union and form the Confederate States of America.

Under President Abraham Lincoln, the North resisted this move and war broke out in 1861. The four-year Civil War that followed divided families and inflicted terrible casualties. In 1865, the North was victorious. The South had lost all its wealth and was now ruined and resentful. The slaves were freed and the Union was preserved.

A Union soldier (from the northern states) in the Civil War.

The United States of America in 1861 at the outbreak of the war between North and South.

FIND OUT MORE

Colonizing America	◄ 40
American Indians	◄ 41
Slavery	◄ 50

See above pages for more information.

THE END OF THE 19TH CENTURY

Although bitterness deepened between the North and the South, the second half of the 19th century was prosperous for the United States. The huge area of the West was settled and immigrants from Europe swelled the population from 31.3 million to 91.9 million. Fortunes were made in banking, manufacturing, railways, mining and steel, so that many individuals became very rich. The United States entered the 20th century as a major industrial power.

A 19th century railroad engine. Railroads were built across America, helping the population to spread across the West.

COLONIAL FEVER

Following the great voyages of the late 15th and 16th centuries, European nations had set up colonies in the Americas. In Africa and Asia, they had been content just to set up trading posts on the coasts. In later centuries, they extended their control over the interiors.

Colonists introduced their own money and stamps, like this British one from South Africa.

British officers in 18th century India. India was Britain's most valuable territory.

AUSTRALIA

Early in the 18th century, Europeans could not see any value in owning colonies abroad. This attitude was shown by the British government, which used Australia as a place to send its criminals. Between 1788 and 1868, 167,000 convicts were sent to Australia. After this, a change in policy brought other settlers seeking their fortunes and a better life in a new land.

EMPIRES ABROAD

As the 18th century progressed, Europeans realized that having colonies around the globe was an advantage. Colonies could act as bases for navies and they could also supply Europe with goods and the raw materials that it needed for manufacturing in the new factories in Europe.

People explored the unknown interiors of Africa and also Australia. By the 19th century, a scramble began to capture colonies abroad. Soldiers, sailors and administrators all became involved in conquering and running huge empires.

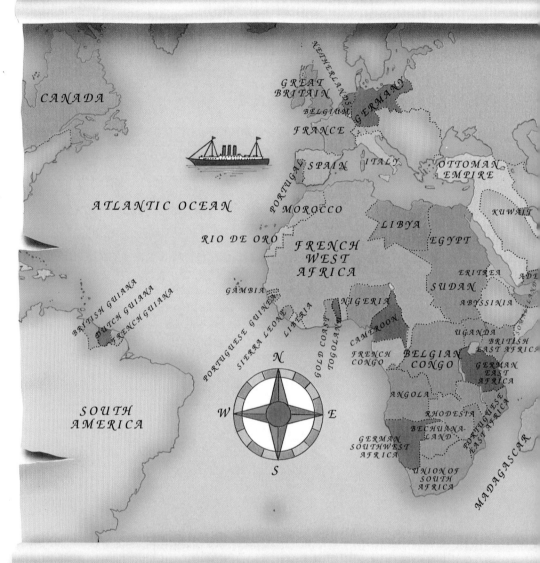

European-style buildings were set up in the African and Asian colonies. This is a Dutch colonial house in the West Indies.

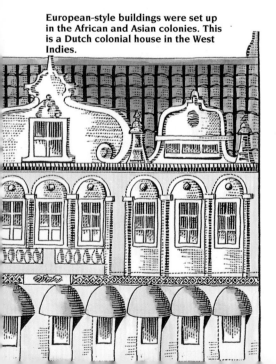

SETTLERS AND NATIVES

After the Industrial Revolution, Europe's population increased rapidly. Some people made huge fortunes, but most were very poor. Going to the colonies was one way that the poor could make a new life. Cheap or free land was available in Africa, Australia, New Zealand and Canada, which had small native populations.

Some natives resented the new arrivals. This led to wars, such as the Zulu Wars in Africa in 1879. Europeans often tried to change the natives' customs and convert them to Christianity, leading to outbreaks of violence such as the Indian Mutiny in 1857-58.

A Zulu shield. The Zulus defeated the British in 1879, in southeast Africa.

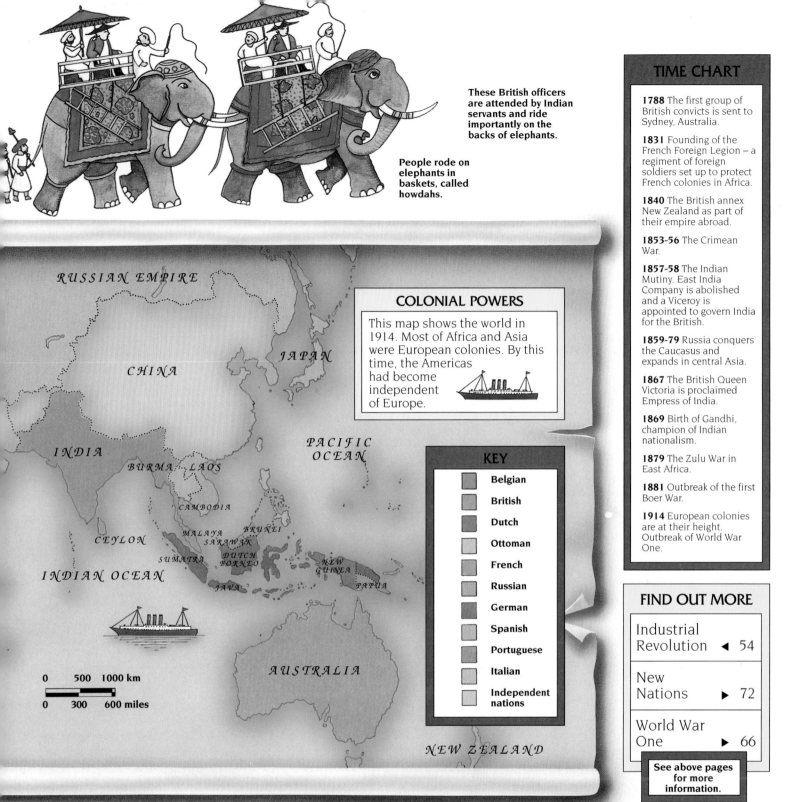

These British officers are attended by Indian servants and ride importantly on the backs of elephants.

People rode on elephants in baskets, called howdahs.

COLONIAL POWERS

This map shows the world in 1914. Most of Africa and Asia were European colonies. By this time, the Americas had become independent of Europe.

KEY

- Belgian
- British
- Dutch
- Ottoman
- French
- Russian
- German
- Spanish
- Portuguese
- Italian
- Independent nations

RUSSIAN EMPIRE

CHINA

JAPAN

INDIA

BURMA LAOS

CAMBODIA

CEYLON

MALAYA BRUNEI
SARAWAK

SUMATRA DUTCH
BORNEO

NEW
GUINEA

PAPUA

JAVA

PACIFIC
OCEAN

INDIAN OCEAN

AUSTRALIA

NEW ZEALAND

0   500   1000 km
0   300   600 miles

TIME CHART

1788 The first group of British convicts is sent to Sydney, Australia.

1831 Founding of the French Foreign Legion – a regiment of foreign soldiers set up to protect French colonies in Africa.

1840 The British annex New Zealand as part of their empire abroad.

1853-56 The Crimean War.

1857-58 The Indian Mutiny. East India Company is abolished and a Viceroy is appointed to govern India for the British.

1859-79 Russia conquers the Caucasus and expands in central Asia.

1867 The British Queen Victoria is proclaimed Empress of India.

1869 Birth of Gandhi, champion of Indian nationalism.

1879 The Zulu War in East Africa.

1881 Outbreak of the first Boer War.

1914 European colonies are at their height. Outbreak of World War One.

FIND OUT MORE

Industrial Revolution	◄ 54
New Nations	► 72
World War One	► 66

See above pages for more information.

ITALY AND GERMANY

In the mid-19th century, Italy and Germany were both made up of lots of separate states. Then in 1861, the Italian states united together to become one country. In 1871 the German states united too. By this time, the other European nations had acquired much territory abroad. Germany and Italy, however, had fallen behind in the race to gain colonies and wealth.

Both Italy and Germany very much resented the fact that they had fallen behind. This created tension in Europe, especially between Germany and its two main rivals, Britain and France. The major European powers became very competitive and this led to an arms race between them. This was one of the causes which led to the outbreak of World War One in 1914.

THE RUSSIAN EMPIRE ABROAD

In the 19th century, Russia extended its territory too. It did not gain colonies overseas, but pushed forward its existing borders. It expanded south into the Khanates – regions controlled by Muslim Turks.

Russia also wanted influence in Christian lands within the Turkish Empire. This resulted in the outbreak of the Crimean War of 1854-56. The British and the French fought as allies of the Turks against the Russians, who lost.

A nurse in the Crimean War – one of the first wars in which women officially served as nurses.

63

THE EARLY 1900s

At the turn of the century, European powers were still colonizing the world and were competing with each other for wealth and territory. Their rivalry led to tensions, both abroad in the colonies and in Europe. At this time, both the United States and Japan were keen to gain territory and influence with other nations.

Japanese soldiers of the Russo-Japanese War of 1904-05.

The last Emperor of China, Pu Yi, who was deposed in 1911.

THE BOER WAR

In the early years of the 20th century, Cape Colony and Natal in southern Africa were British colonies. Many Europeans lived there. Among them were the Boers, descendants of Dutch colonists, who were fiercely independent. In 1899 a war had broken out between the Boers and the British, who had expanded into Boer territory.

The Queen's South Africa Medal, awarded to British soldiers who fought in the Boer War.

In 1902, after brutal fighting, Britain declared victory. A new state was created called the Union of South Africa, which aimed to reconcile the British and the Boers.

Cape Colony and Natal in 1830. Europeans settled here when they first arrived to colonize southern Africa.

The Boers created Transvaal and the Orange Free State in the 1850s. The British later expanded into these areas.

The Union of South Africa. This new state was created after peace was declared in 1902.

JAPAN EXPANDS

In 1904, a war broke out between Russia and Japan called the Russo-Japanese War. Japan won, which was the first time in centuries that an Asian power had beaten a European one. Encouraged by its success, Japan then invaded China.

The Chinese could do little to stop Japanese expansion. China itself was in turmoil. The government was very weak and warlords commanded their own territories. To stabilize China, rebels wanted to get rid of the Manchu Emperor Pu Yi, whose family had ruled for centuries. He was only six years old and his government was near to collapse. In 1911, Pu Yi was deposed and China became a republic, led by Dr. Sun Yat Sen.

Boer farmers who fought the British in 1899-1902. This picture shows three generations of the same family.

Russian territory in 1904. The Russians occupied parts of Manchuria in China and also, briefly, Korea.

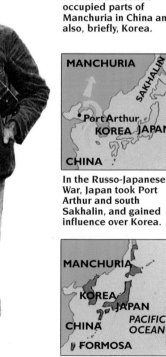

In the Russo-Japanese War, Japan took Port Arthur and south Sakhalin, and gained influence over Korea.

Japanese territory in 1910. By this time Japan was in control of Korea and Formosa (now Taiwan).

THE USA

Like other world powers, the USA also had ambitions to influence world affairs. In 1903, the USA encouraged Panama to rebel against its rulers, Colombia. It invested money in Panama to buy land and help build the Panama Canal. The USA hoped to benefit from the extra trade that the canal would bring to the region.

The rest of Central America was unstable too. By promising economic and military support, the USA managed to bring Nicaragua, Cuba, the Dominican Republic and Haiti under its influence.

EUROPE IN TURMOIL

In 1904, France and Germany had a dispute. This arose because Britain and France had agreed that France should have control over the African country of Morocco. The German Kaiser Wilhelm II was furious that he had not been consulted and demanded a conference on the subject. At the conference, other nations supported France. Germany began to feel that Europe was against it. Europe was becoming dangerously unstable when more trouble followed in the Balkan Wars of 1912-13.

During the Balkan Wars, Serbia, Greece, Bulgaria and Montenegro banded together to push the weak Ottoman Empire out of Europe. However, the victors then fought over the control of their new territory. Bulgaria lost and Serbia gained more territory. Serbia became a strong power, which made Austria and Germany nervous. Meanwhile, France promised to back Russia, Serbia's ally, against any German aggression. European powers split into two camps and the stage was set for war.

THE ARMS RACE

Germany and Britain were great rivals. Both had strong industries and Britain wanted to maintain its position as a dominant world power. After the Morocco crisis, Germany decided to build a great navy and Britain began to modernize its fleet. They tried to outdo each other by building bigger and better ships.

The result was a race in which both nations built up their navies and arms supplies. They were deeply suspicious of one another. This arms race was one of the causes of World War One.

Areas of US political influence in Central America and the Caribbean in the early 1900s.

The Balkan countries at the outbreak of the Balkan Wars in 1912.

The new borders of the Balkan countries on the eve of World War One in 1914.

TIME CHART

1899-1902 The Boer War.

1903 The USA signs an everlasting lease for the site of the Panama Canal.

1904-05 The Russo-Japanese War.

1904-14 The building of the Panama Canal.

1905 Widespread rebellions against the Tsar take place in Russia. Kaiser Wilhelm II of Germany protests against French control of Morocco.

1906 Nations debate the Morocco problem at a conference in Algeçiras, Spain.

1908 Army officers revolt in the Ottoman Empire. The Austro-Hungarian Empire takes Bosnia from the Ottomans.

1910 The Union of South Africa becomes a British dominion.

1911 French forces take the city of Fez in Morocco. Germans send a gun boat to Morocco to threaten the French. Emperor Pu Yi of China is deposed and a republic is set up there.

1912 The Italians take Libya from the Ottomans. The First Balkan War.

1913 The Second Balkan War.

1913-14 European nations build up their armed forces.

FIND OUT MORE

China	◄	48
Japan	◄	52
World War One	►	66

See above pages for more information.

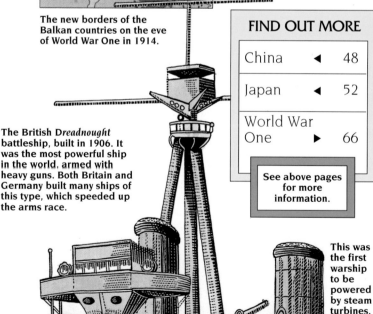

The British *Dreadnought* battleship, built in 1906. It was the most powerful ship in the world, armed with heavy guns. Both Britain and Germany built many ships of this type, which speeded up the arms race.

The *Dreadnought* was heavily built with a double bottom to withstand attacks from torpedoes.

Battleships of the *Dreadnought* type were armed with big, 30cm (12in) guns.

This was the first warship to be powered by steam turbines.

WORLD WAR ONE

In 1914, tensions were high between the dominant European nations of Germany, France, Britain and Russia. At this time, Serbia wanted independence for Serb people who were part of the Austria-Hungary Empire, but Austria would not allow it.

George V, King of England during World War One. He reigned from 1910-36.

Kaiser Wilhelm II of Germany was George V's first cousin. He reigned from 1888-1918.

HOW THE WAR BEGAN

On June 28, 1914, the Archduke Franz Ferdinand, heir to the Austrian Empire, was on a royal visit to Sarajevo in Bosnia. A Serbian terrorist gang was waiting for him and as he drove through the streets, the Archduke was suddenly shot dead. Austria, with Germany's backing, ordered Serbia to bring the murderers to justice. Serbia refused to agree with all of Austria's demands, so on July 28, Austria declared war on Serbia. Serbia, however, had a powerful friend to support it – Russia.

Next, Russia moved its troops towards Austria. Germany then saw its chance to declare war on Russia and also on Russia's ally, France. The German army's first move in the war was to invade France. Their route took them into Belgium, which outraged the British, who had promised to defend Belgian neutrality. So Britain declared war on Germany. Europe was now divided: Britain, France and Russia, called the Allies, against Germany and Austria, called the Central Powers.

Austria had recently annexed Bosnia and Herzegovina. This infuriated the Serbians in Bosnia, who wanted to be independent.

Sarajevo was the capital of Bosnia and Herzegovina. It was here that the heir to the throne of Austria-Hungary was shot in 1914.

Germany took the opportunity to invade its old enemy, France. The invasion route took German forces through neutral Belgium.

Europe was now split in two camps – Austria and Germany, the Central Powers, versus Britain, France and Russia – the Allies.

FIGHTING AT THE FRONTS

The area of fighting in France and Belgium was called the Western Front. Both sides expected a quick victory, but the German attack was stopped at the Marne River, and the Allies were stopped at Ypres. Soldiers on both sides dug trenches for protection against bombardment from heavy guns and machine gun fire. They attacked by charging across muddy open ground, through barbed wire entanglements. Poison gas was also used as a weapon.

Germany's plan was to defeat France quickly and then fight the Russian army after that. This plan failed and Germany could not crack French resistance to their attack. So it was now forced to fight Russia in the east at the same time as France in the west. The area where fighting between the Germans and the Russians took place is called the Eastern Front. The German attack was stopped in 1915, creating another hopeless stalemate.

The Western Front in 1915. Heavy fighting took place along the French borders throughout the First World War.

In May 1915, Italy joined the Allies. However, fighting near the border between Italy and Austria-Hungary developed into another stalemate.

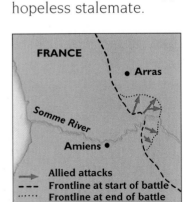

In 1916, the Allies attacked across the Somme River. This battle raged for six months, but ended with the Allies gaining little ground.

The Eastern Front in 1915. Troops fought along a line that stretched from the Baltic Sea in the north to the Ukraine in the south.

THE WAR SPREADS

During the war, other nations decided to join either the Allies or the Central Powers, according to which side they thought might benefit them. As well as Italy, Japan joined the Allies, while Turkey joined the Central Powers. The war involved more nations than any war before. Fighting also spread outside Europe to German colonies in Africa and to the Turkish Empire.

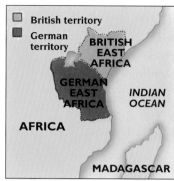

- British territory
- German territory

BRITISH EAST AFRICA
GERMAN EAST AFRICA
INDIAN OCEAN
AFRICA
MADAGASCAR

Fighting took place in the European colonies of British and German East Africa. At the end of the war, Britain gained German East Africa.

- Ottoman territory

TURKEY
OTTOMAN EMPIRE
CASPIAN SEA
PALESTINE
MESOPOTAMIA
ARABIA
RED SEA
PERSIAN GULF

Allied troops fought the Turks in Palestine and Mesopotamia. The Arabs revolted against Ottoman rule and also fought the Turks.

USA IN, RUSSIA OUT

Germany began to use submarines, or U-Boats, to torpedo supply ships in the Atlantic. American ships were sunk, which angered the USA. It joined the Allies in 1917. Russia, however, found that it could fight no longer. A group called the Bolsheviks took power and made peace with Germany. Germany now had to crush Britain and France before the Americans arrived.

NORTH AMERICA
EUROPE
ATLANTIC OCEAN
AFRICA
SOUTH AMERICA
INDIAN OCEAN

➤ Supply route

British supply routes in the Atlantic. German U-Boats torpedoed ships to prevent Britain getting food and supplies from other countries.

✦ U-Boat sinkings

SCANDINAVIA
ATLANTIC OCEAN
GREAT BRITAIN
EUROPE
MEDITERRANEAN SEA
AFRICA

Hundreds of U-Boats were also sunk around the coast of Britain and northern France throughout the duration of the war.

THE FIGHTING STOPS

In 1918, the German army made another attack on the Western Front. However, now they were fighting against fresh American troops and also against tanks – a new weapon. A defeat at Amiens led to Germans calling for the war to end. On November 9, the Kaiser abdicated and on November 11 an end to the fighting, or armistice, was agreed. At last, fighting stopped on the Western Front. In all, 65 million men fought, of whom 10 million were killed and 20 million injured.

A British Mark IV tank, as used in World War One. This was the first war ever in which tanks were used.

Caterpillar tracks helped the tank move across muddy fields.

Poppies that grew on the battlefields of the Western Front became a symbol of remembrance.

Inside early tanks like this one was an eight man crew – the commander, four gunners, a driver and two gearsmen, who helped operate the tank.

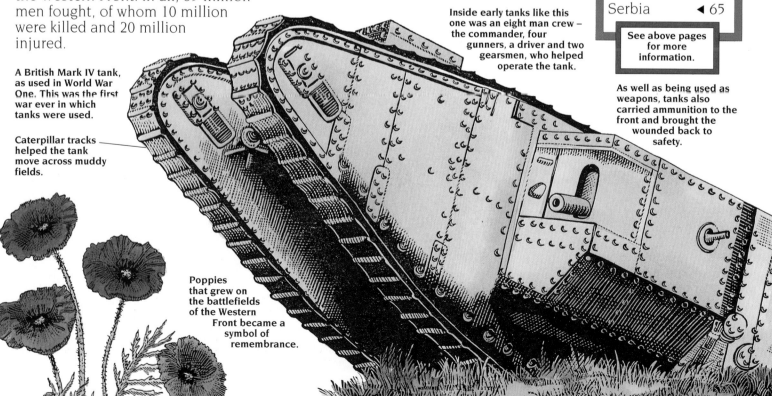

As well as being used as weapons, tanks also carried ammunition to the front and brought the wounded back to safety.

TIME CHART

June 28, 1914 Archduke Franz Ferdinand is shot dead in Sarajevo.

July 28, 1914 Austria declares war on Serbia.

August 1914 Germany declares war on Russia and France. Britain declares war on Germany. Japan joins the Allies.

November 1914 The Ottoman Empire joins the Central Powers.

May 1915 Italy joins the Allies.

September 1915 Bulgaria joins the Central Powers.

March 1916 Portugal joins the Allies.

August 1916 Romania joins the Allies.

March 15, 1917 The Russian Tsar abdicates.

April 6, 1917 USA declares war on Germany.

June 1917 Greece joins the Allies.

October 24-25, 1917 Bolsheviks seize power in the Russian Revolution.

March 3, 1918 Russia and Germany sign a peace treaty of Brest-Litovsk.

November 9, 1918 Kaiser Wilhelm II abdicates.

November 11, 1918 Armistice declared.

BETWEEN THE WARS

In 1919, a peace conference in Paris tried to form a peace settlement after World War One. It took six months to make a treaty, called the Treaty of Versailles. Germany had to hand over territory and efforts were made to make it pay for the damage caused. Austria and Turkey both lost their empires.

The flag of the communist Soviet Union.

THE LEAGUE OF NATIONS

The US president, Woodrow Wilson, suggested that an international organization should be set up to prevent war. This organization was called the League of Nations.

The USA itself, however, did not join the League of Nations. This was because its government did not want to be involved in Europe's affairs. The Soviet Union did not attend the conference in Paris and neither did it join the League at first. So, two of the most important powers in the world were not members, which made the League of Nations weak.

COMMUNIST RUSSIA

After the Russian Revolution in 1917, the Bolsheviks took over the old Russian Empire. They set up a communist government, which was based on providing equality and state control of people's everyday lives.

This new state was called the Soviet Union, or USSR. When its leader Lenin died, Josef Stalin took power. He wanted to make the Soviet Union great and he did this by building railways and factories. To do this, he took much land away from the peasants and many people died of starvation or were sent to harsh work camps.

An unemployed man from the USA. The unemployed protested about the lack of work.

Josef Stalin, the Soviet leader. He ruled from 1929 until his death in 1953.

HITLER'S GERMANY

In 1929 the US stock market crashed, which meant that many people lost money and businesses went bankrupt. During the 1930s, many people were poor and unemployment was high. This period was known as the Great Depression.

Germany was badly affected by the Great Depression and by the aftermath of World War One. Adolf Hitler, the head of the National Socialist German Workers Party, or Nazi Party, persuaded the German people that their troubles were caused by foreigners, especially Jews. As a result, during the 1930s, German Jews were persecuted. Hitler's party won popular support. He was a persuasive speaker and soon he became a powerful politician.

In 1933 the German President made Hitler the Chancellor. He later became the outright leader, or Führer. Hitler planned to dominate Europe and in 1938, his troops marched into Austria to achieve the Anschluss – the joining of Austria and Germany.

Austria became part of a German Empire which became known as the Third Reich. Before long, Germany's attempts to extend this empire led to World War Two.

A 1930s German propaganda booklet, designed to persuade people to follow Hitler. The words on the cover mean "Children, what do you know about your Führer?"

Northern Ireland (or Ulster) remained part of Great Britain.

NORTHERN IRELAND

IRISH FREE STATE

GREAT BRITAIN

The Irish Free State became independent from Great Britain in 1922.

0   500 km

0   300 miles

From 1936-39, Communists fought Fascists for control of Spain. The Fascists won under General Franco.

SPAIN

PORTUGAL

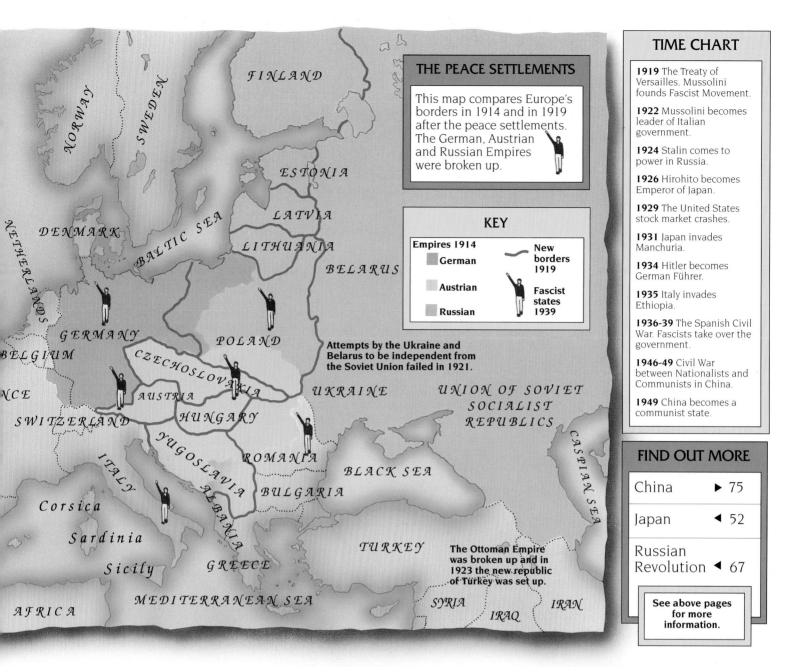

THE PEACE SETTLEMENTS

This map compares Europe's borders in 1914 and in 1919 after the peace settlements. The German, Austrian and Russian Empires were broken up.

KEY

Empires 1914	
German	⌇ New borders 1919
Austrian	🙋 Fascist states 1939
Russian	

Attempts by the Ukraine and Belarus to be independent from the Soviet Union failed in 1921.

The Ottoman Empire was broken up and in 1923 the new republic of Turkey was set up.

TIME CHART

1919 The Treaty of Versailles. Mussolini founds Fascist Movement.

1922 Mussolini becomes leader of Italian government.

1924 Stalin comes to power in Russia.

1926 Hirohito becomes Emperor of Japan.

1929 The United States stock market crashes.

1931 Japan invades Manchuria.

1934 Hitler becomes German Führer.

1935 Italy invades Ethiopia.

1936-39 The Spanish Civil War. Fascists take over the government.

1946-49 Civil War between Nationalists and Communists in China.

1949 China becomes a communist state.

FIND OUT MORE

China	▶ 75
Japan	◀ 52
Russian Revolution	◀ 67

See above pages for more information.

FASCIST ITALY

In the 1920s, a man called Benito Mussolini became powerful in Italy. He belonged to a political group called the Fascists which, like the Nazi Party and the Communists, also believed in a strong government. Mussolini became a dictator, ruling Italy by force and by his ideas alone.

By the mid-1930s, his ideas were clearly not working. So, in a bid for popularity with the Italian people, his army invaded Ethiopia in Africa. The League of Nations could do very little to stop him. Its actions irritated Mussolini, bringing him closer to Hitler.

The Fascist symbol – the *fasces* ("bundle of rods"). It was originally an Ancient Roman symbol of authority.

TENSIONS IN ASIA

In 1926 Emperor Hirohito came to the throne in Japan. After this Japan became more aggressive to other countries. The emperor took advice from military leaders, including the Prime Minister, General Tanaka, who wanted to build a Japanese Empire in Asia.

In 1931, Japan invaded Manchuria in China and set up a new state called Manchukuo. Manchukuo was controlled directly by Japan. The League of Nations was against the invasion, but Japan responded by leaving the League.

It then signed a pact with Nazi Germany and started a war with China. This left Japan ruling part of China itself. Tensions grew steadily and the world sank deeper into a crisis.

COMMUNIST CHINA

Founded in 1921, the Chinese Communist Party wanted to improve conditions and free China from Japanese domination. After the war with Japan, it grabbed power, causing a civil war. The communists were eventually victorious and China became a communist state in 1949.

Mao Zedong, leader of the Chinese Communist Party from 1936 until 1976, when he died.

WORLD WAR TWO

German bombers, called Heinkel One-Elevens.

In the 1930s, Hitler, the German Nazi leader, wanted to create one state for all German people. Germany had forced Austria into a union, in an event called the Anschluss. Now Germany and its allies, called the Axis Powers, set out to create a German empire in Europe.

Nazi salute.

THE INVASIONS BEGIN

Hitler's first target was the Sudetenland – an area of Czechoslovakia. Britain and France, anxious to avoid war, agreed that this area should join with Germany. Soon though, the Nazis occupied the whole of Czechoslovakia. Hitler then invaded Poland on September 1, 1939. This time, Britain and France had no choice but to declare war. On September 17 the Soviets, allied with Hitler, invaded Poland too.

Before the war began, Germany's allies were Bulgaria, Hungary and Romania. Together they were called the Axis Powers.

Germany had occupied the Sudetenland by October 1938. By March 1939, the rest of Czechoslovakia was under German occupation.

By September 28, 1939, Poland was beaten. German and Russian troops met in Poland on the line agreed by their leaders.

THE WAR IN EUROPE

Benito Mussolini, the Italian leader and Hitler's ally.

In 1940, Germany occupied Norway and Denmark, then stormed across the Netherlands, Belgium and France, using a tactic called Blitzkrieg ("lightning war"). France had to surrender but Britain and the Allies (New Zealand, Australia, Canada, and South Africa) fought on.

Norway and Denmark held important positions on the North Atlantic coast. In April 1940, both countries were invaded by Germany.

The German army moved east and the British forces escaped by sea from Dunkirk. In June, France made peace with Germany.

Vichy-France was run by a French government based at Vichy under orders from the Nazis. Northern France was occupied by Germany.

AIR AND SEA

Although Allied troops were defeated in Europe, Hitler failed to win supremacy in an air battle, called the Battle of Britain, which took place over southern England. Hitler also tried to break Britain's supply routes across the sea, but his submarines (or U-Boats) were eventually defeated in the long Battle of the Atlantic.

Allied fighter planes were stationed all over southern Britain. Axis fighters were stationed in northern France.

Germany began to lose the Battle of Britain, so Hitler began to bomb British cities, shown above, in an attack called the Blitz.

Throughout the war, German cities were also bombed by the Allies. The above cities were very severely damaged.

THE WAR SPREADS

In mid 1940, Italy's leader Mussolini, joined the Axis Powers. Italy's first move was to invade Greece. It then attacked the British in Egypt from its own colony of Libya. However, the Italians were pushed back and German forces had to rescue them by invading Greece, Yugoslavia and North Africa.

The Germans and their Bulgarian allies staged a joint invasion of Yugoslavia and Greece on April 6, 1941.

German troops landed in Libya in February 1941. They attacked toward the British in Egypt who were defending the Suez Canal.

After an important battle at El Alamein, the Axis Powers retreated to Tunis. Surrounded by the Allies, they surrendered in 1943.

THE SOVIET UNION

Although Germany and the Soviets had signed a pact, in 1941 German troops made a surprise attack on the Soviet Union. They moved quickly but the harsh winter was beginning and Soviet resistance was fierce. Germany lost many men and morale was low.

Some Soviet troops were equipped with skis in the winter.

On June 22, 1941, Axis troops attacked the Soviet Union from Poland, Hungary, Romania and Prussia.

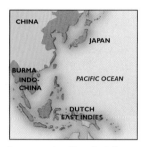

In 1939, the Soviet Union had occupied territory in Finland. Now the Finns fought back on Germany's side.

By December 1941, the Germans had advanced almost to Moscow. Soviet resistance stopped them from advancing any more.

PEARL HARBOR

In 1940, tension between Japan and the USA was high, due to Japan's recent territorial gains in the Pacific. Worse still, Japan signed a pact with the Axis Powers. Suddenly in December 1941, it made a devastating air attack on the US naval base at Pearl Harbor in Hawaii. In outrage, the USA joined the Allies in the war, but not before Japan had managed to conquer a lot of territory in the Pacific.

→ Japanese air attack

Many US warships were in Pearl Harbor on the Hawaiian island of Oahu when the Japanese attacked on December 7.

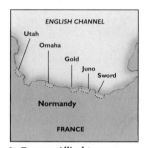

Japanese territory in July 1942. By this time, Japan had occupied territory in Burma, China, Indo-China and the Dutch East Indies.

✳ Naval battles

The naval fleets of Japan and the USA fought the above battles in the Pacific. By the end of 1942, Japan was losing.

THE WAR ENDS – 1945

In 1943 and 1944, the Allies landed troops in Italy and France. As they advanced, the Soviets attacked Germany from the east. Facing certain defeat, Hitler killed himself and Germany surrendered. In the Pacific, though the Allies gradually won back lost territory, Japan did not surrender until atomic bombs had been dropped on Nagasaki and Hiroshima, causing terrible destruction and loss of life.

Allied invasion

The Allied invasion of Italy began in July 1943 and Mussolini fell from power shortly after. In June 1944, the Allies entered Rome.

In France, Allied troops invaded Normandy. The five beaches where they landed were given the above codenames.

As the war drew to an end, the Soviets and the Allies closed in on Berlin. The Soviets reached the German capital first.

THE HOLOCAUST

A Jewish child surrenders to a German soldier.

As the war ended, it became clear that something evil had happened. Hitler had hated Jews, blaming them for Germany's problems. He had set up concentration camps, where millions of Jews and other people classed as undesirable by the Nazis, were killed. This event is called the Holocaust, meaning a total destruction of life.

△ Concentration camp

Concentration camps, where mass murders took place, were situated in the above places in central Europe.

These buildings, like those in many German cities, were almost totally destroyed by bombs.

TIME CHART

March 1939 Germany gains control of Czechoslovakia.

September 1, 1939 Germany invades Poland.

September 3, 1939 Britain and France declare war on Germany.

April-May 1940 Germany stages invasions across western Europe.

May 1940 Allies evacuate 300,000 troops from Dunkirk in France.

April 1941 Germany occupies Greece and Yugoslavia. Fighting starts in North Africa.

June 22, 1941 Germany invades the Soviet Union.

September 1943 Italy surrenders to the Allies.

June 6, 1944 Allied invasion of Normandy, codenamed D-Day.

May 8, 1945 Germany surrenders.

August 1945 Hiroshima and Nagasaki are devastated by atomic bombs.

August 14, 1945 Japan surrenders, ending the war.

NEW NATIONS

The symbol of the United Nations – formed in 1945 to tackle world problems.

After World War Two, Europe was nearly bankrupt and could no longer maintain its colonial empires. The colonies wanted self-government and a period began when many of them gained independence.

The flag of Israel – the first new nation created after World War Two.

ISRAEL IS BORN

After the war, a new organization called the United Nations was set up to settle disagreements between nations and to prevent war breaking out again. One of the first problems it had to tackle was a crisis in Palestine in the Middle East. During the 20th century, great numbers of Jews had arrived in Palestine, which they saw as their traditional homeland. However, the Arab Palestinians resisted the arrival of Jews in the area that was their homeland too. In 1948, the United Nations came up with a solution – the creation of a new Jewish state of Israel in Palestine. The Palestinians soon became a nation without a home and years of violence between Jews and Arabs followed.

Israel in 1949, after a War of Independence with the surrounding Arab countries.

War broke out in 1967 and Israel gained more territory. It returned the Sinai Peninsula to Egypt in 1982.

INDIAN INDEPENDENCE

Before World War Two, political groups in India campaigned for independence from Britain. A group called Congress, led by Mahatma Gandhi, was the main group. However, a second group, called the Muslim League, wanted a separate state for Muslims. Another group, called the Sikhs, wanted a state too.

In 1947, the British made India independent, but also created a separate Muslim state – Pakistan. Thousands died in violence as Muslims moved from Hindu areas and vice-versa. Among all this turmoil, no state was created for the Sikhs.

WAR IN INDOCHINA

During World War Two, French Indochina had been occupied by Japan. A resistance group had been formed to fight them and now that the war was over, they were reluctant to let the French govern. As demands for independence spread across Asia, resistance fighters began a guerilla war against the French.

By 1954, it was all-out war. After a bad defeat at Dien Bien Phu, France decided to pull out. Laos and Cambodia became independent, but Vietnam was temporarily split into two zones. Communists dominated the north, while a government friendly to the USA ran the south.

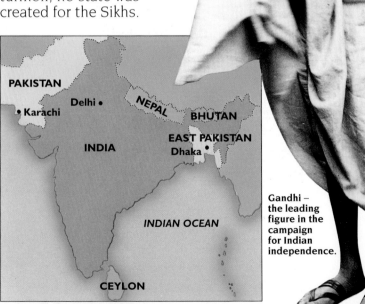

Gandhi – the leading figure in the campaign for Indian independence.

The Indian continent in 1947. East Pakistan became Bangladesh in 1971 and Ceylon became Sri Lanka in 1972.

In 1953-54, French Indochina split into Cambodia, Laos and North and South Vietnam.

This map shows the newly independent countries and their new flags at the time of their independence.

INDEPENDENCE IN AFRICA

African countries began to demand their freedom too. One country after another became successful, including Nigeria, which was the richest colony. On independence, many new states joined the British Commonwealth or the French Community – associations of states that were once British or French colonies.

0 — 1000 km
0 — 500 miles

TIME CHART

1947 India becomes independent. East and West Pakistan are created.

1948 Israel becomes a nation. The first Arab-Israeli war takes place. Gandhi is assassinated in India. The National Party comes to power in South Africa.

1949 The Dutch give up control of Indonesia.

1954 Indochina wins independence from France.

1958-62 Algerian War of Independence against France takes place.

1960 Nigeria becomes independent.

1960-64 Fighting takes place in the Congo.

1961 Angola rebels against Portugal. South Africa leaves the British Commonwealth.

1962 Mozambique rebels against Portugal.

1964 Army mutinies take place in Kenya and Uganda.

1965 Rhodesia declares independence.

1975 Angola and Mozambique become independent. Civil war follows.

1980 Rhodesia becomes Zimbabwe.

Liberia was never colonized. It was created by the USA as a state for free slaves in 1821.

KEY TO INDEPENDENCE DATES

1. Algeria 1962
2. Angola 1975
3. Botswana 1966
4. Burundi 1962
5. Cameroon 1960
6. Central African Rep. 1960
7. Chad 1960
8. Congo 1960
9. Dahomey 1960
10. Djibouti 1977
11. Egypt – not colonized
12. Equatorial Guinea 1968
13. Ethiopia 1941
14. Gabon 1960
15. Gambia 1965
16. Ghana 1957
17. Guinea 1958
18. Guinea Bissau 1973
19. Ivory Coast 1960
20. Kenya 1963
21. Lesotho 1966
22. Liberia – not colonized
23. Libya 1951
24. Madagascar 1960
25. Malawi 1964
26. Mali 1960
27. Mauritania 1960
28. Morocco 1956
29. Mozambique 1975
30. Namibia 1990
31. Niger 1960
32. Nigeria 1960
33. Rhodesia 1965
34. Rwanda 1962
35. Senegal 1960
36. Sierra Leone 1961
37. Somalia 1960
38. South Africa 1961
39. Sudan 1956
40. Swaziland 1968
41. Tanzania 1961
42. Togo 1960
43. Tunisia 1956
44. Uganda 1962
45. Upper Volta 1960
46. Zaire 1960
47. Zambia 1964

FIND OUT MORE

Colonies ◀ 62

Communism ◀ 68

See above pages for more information

South Africa was part of the British Commonwealth until 1961, when it became an independent republic.

APARTHEID

In 1948, the National Party came to power in South Africa. It set up a system which kept advantages for white people, while nonwhite people had few rights. This system was called apartheid. As more African countries joined the British Commonwealth, they put pressure on Britain to force South Africa to give everyone the same rights. South Africa refused to change and responded by leaving the Commonwealth in 1961.

NEW STATES IN TROUBLE

Tension between rival groups and lack of political experience made some states unstable. In the Belgian Congo, anger over former ill-treatment led to attacks against whites. In Angola and Mozambique, independence led to civil wars. In Rhodesia, a white government refused to hand over power to the black majority, which led to years of protest. Finally in 1980, Rhodesia became Zimbabwe – a new state with a black majority government.

During the civil war in Mozambique, this boy is being taught how to use a rocket launcher.

THE COLD WAR

Built in 1961, the Berlin wall split the city into communist East and the free West.

After World War Two, the Soviet Union and the USA were very suspicious of each other. Their relationship became so bad that it developed into a cold war – a war of economics and politics, rather than actual fighting. Both sides stockpiled nuclear weapons.

In 1989, the Berlin Wall was taken down. Here, joyous Berliners help to dismantle it.

TAKING SIDES

After World War Two, the USA and the Soviet Union became known as the superpowers, because they were the strongest countries in the world. During the Cold War, communist countries tended to be backed and influenced by the Soviet Union. Other countries, such as those in Western Europe, were backed by the USA. This division caused great suspicion between communist and non-communist countries.

China was an exception. Although it had a communist government, it was not friendly with either the Soviet Union or the USA.

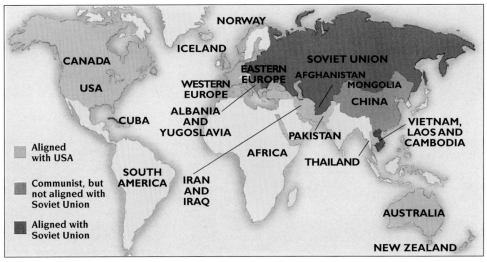

Aligned with USA

Communist, but not aligned with Soviet Union

Aligned with Soviet Union

During the Cold War, many countries of the world had treaties with either the USA or the Soviet Union. This map shows which parts of the world were allies of which superpower.

THE IRON CURTAIN

After the war, communist parties came to power in Czechoslovakia, Hungary, Poland and other Eastern European countries. To help Europe recover from the war, the USA offered money in a scheme called the Marshall Plan. However, while Western Europe accepted aid, the Soviet Union did not allow Eastern Europe to do so.

As the two halves of Europe grew apart, the ex-Prime Minister of Britain, Winston Churchill, described this separation as an "Iron Curtain" coming down to divide Europe. This phrase came to describe the division between the two sides in the Cold War.

A German "Marshall Plan" poster. This scheme gave US economic help to Europe.

Eastern Europe in 1949. By this time, all nations in Eastern Europe were Communist and most were influenced by the Soviet Union.

GERMANY DIVIDES

After the war, Germany had been divided into four zones – Soviet, American, British and French. The capital Berlin, in the middle of the Soviet zone, was itself split into east and west. By 1947, Germany was operating as two countries. In October 1949, it officially became two countries – East and West Germany. People began to try to leave the East for the West and the easiest route was between East and West Berlin. This was embarrassing for the Soviet Union, so in 1961 soldiers built a wall almost overnight, dividing the city. The Berlin Wall became a symbol of the Cold War.

Germany after the war. Both it and its capital Berlin were divided into four zones. The Soviet zone later became East Germany.

One of the many observation towers which guarded the Berlin Wall.

CUBA

As the Cold War progressed, each side began to build up their weapons. In 1962, a serious threat to peace erupted over Cuba. Cuba's leader, Fidel Castro, was friendly with the Soviet Union, which now announced that it planned to use Cuba as a base for its nuclear missiles. This move greatly alarmed the USA, which felt threatened.

Cuba, a Caribbean island just off the coast of Florida, USA. When the Soviet Union wanted to base nuclear missiles here in 1962, the security of the USA was threatened.

The USA began a naval blockade of Cuba, refusing to let Soviet ships approach it. For days the world was on the brink of nuclear war, but eventually the Soviet Union backed down.

KOREA AND VIETNAM

Tensions between communist groups and their opponents caused many conflicts around the world during the Cold War. These included two major wars in East Asia.

In the 1950s, the Korean War erupted, which lasted until 1953. It was followed by the Vietnam War in the 1960s and 70s. This war, involving US soldiers, was a particularly long and bloody conflict.

In 1950, North Korean communists, backed by China, invaded the south. United Nations forces successfully defended the south, resulting in the creation of North and South Korea.

In Vietnam, US troops supported the south against communists, called the Vietcong, in the north. A vicious war resulted in defeat for the USA and Vietnam became communist.

FIND OUT MORE

Communism ◄	68
United Nations	◄ 72

See above pages for more information.

COMMUNIST CHINA

In the late 1960s the Chinese leader, Mao Zedong, decided that China was no longer true to Communist ideals. He encouraged young people to join a group called the Red Guards. Often using violence, the Red Guards forced their teachers and bosses to confess that they were behaving wrongly. During this period, called the Cultural Revolution, schools closed and work was disrupted. Many people died or were imprisoned. In the mid-1970s the Cultural Revolution stopped and when Mao died in 1976, China began to recover.

Chairman Mao Zedong in the 1960s.

THE COLD WAR ENDS

In the 1970s and 80s, the superpowers continued to back groups close to their own ideas. The USA supported revolutions in Chile and Nicaragua, while the Soviets occupied Afghanistan. However, by 1987 the Soviet Union and Eastern Europe had economic problems. Soviet President Gorbachev wanted to end the Cold War. In 1990, it finally seemed to end when the two sides were allies in the Gulf War.

United Nations soldiers of the Korean War.

THE DEVELOPING WORLD

The symbol of UNICEF, which helps children in developing countries.

After gaining independence from European countries, many of the ex-colonies in Asia and Africa were faced with economic and environmental problems. To improve the situation, African and Asian countries began to develop their industry and farming. For this reason, they are known as developing countries.

AID AND WORLD TRADE

In the 1960s and 70s, the USA, the Soviet Union and Europe all gave aid in the form of loans to developing countries. Developing countries had to pay the money back and also pay interest – a borrowing charge. By the end of the 1970s, it was clear that they could not repay the massive loans.

This was partly due to the fact that developing countries were at a disadvantage over trade. They were the main producers of raw materials, such as coffee beans or copper, but earned only small amounts of money from this. The richer, industrial nations earned more money by using the raw materials to manufacture goods, such as instant coffee or copper pipes.

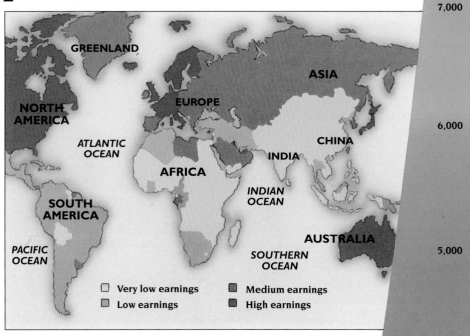

Average earnings per person in each country. The poorest countries are in Africa and Asia.

THE POPULATION EXPLOSION

During the 20th century, there has been an enormous increase in world population. In 1900, there were 1,625 million people in the world. By the mid 1990s, this figure had risen to around 5,000 million people. The population is now growing faster than ever, which is a strain on the world's resources.

Most of the population growth has taken place in less developed countries. This is because in the past people needed large families to help earn a living. Many children died, so people did not want to limit the number of babies that they had. In recent years, health care has improved, so more babies survive, though people are still having large families. This means that poorer countries are having to support more and more people. There is enough food to keep the population growing, but not enough to keep everyone healthy.

In China, couples are allowed to have only one child. This is a Chinese poster, which reminds them of this.

This graph shows how the population of the world has risen since the 14th century. It also predicts how the population might keep growing in the 21st century.

Population (millions)

9,000

8,000

7,000

6,000

5,000

4,000

3,000

2,000

1,000

1300   1400   1500   1600   1700   1800   1900   2000

Date (year)

WAR AND FAMINE

Newly-independent countries are often troubled by political problems, which can end in war. During a war, people may be forced to leave their homes in huge numbers. They flock into nearby regions, hoping to find food and safety. People who have to leave their homes in this way are called refugees.

To make matters worse, since the 1960s there have been several droughts in Africa, when crops could not grow for lack of water. This combined with the effects of wars to create terrible famines, during which there was not enough for people or their farm animals to eat. In turn, famines have created millions of refugees. In 1985, a famine in Ethiopia was highlighted by a huge televized pop concert called Live Aid. The concert raised over 100,000,000 US dollars to help the starving.

A schoolboy in Ethiopia receiving lessons in his local school.

TIME CHART

1961-91 Civil war in Ethiopia.

1967-70 The Biafran conflict in Nigeria.

1970s Intensive clearing of the Amazon Forest begins in Brazil.

1977-78 Ethiopia is at war with Somalia.

1980 The Brandt Report criticizes the world trade system, in which richer countries benefit from trade with poorer ones.

1980s A series of wars and droughts leads to widespread famine in East Africa.

1985 Civil war begins in Sudan.

July, 1985 Live Aid concert is broadcast in Europe and the USA to raise money for famine relief in East Africa.

1991 Civil war begins in Somalia.

September, 1992 The Rio Summit, a huge publicity event to save the environment, takes place in Rio de Janeiro, Brazil.

August 1994 Rwandan Civil War. Millions flee from their homes.

In 1967 in Nigeria, the region of Biafra tried to become independent. Nigeria was opposed to this and a civil war broke out. The fighting led to a famine and 300,000 people became refugees. Nigeria won the war in 1970.

In the 1980s, a series of wars and famines in Somalia, Sudan and Ethiopia created millions of refugees. People from Zaire, Chad and Uganda also crowded into Ethiopia, which could not cope.

In 1994 in Rwanda in central Africa, a civil war broke out. To escape the war, millions walked into nearby Zaire, where there was no food or shelter for them. This created one of the worst refugee problems ever.

FIND OUT MORE

Independence ◀ 72

ENVIRONMENT IN DANGER

In today's world there are many threats to the environment. In developing countries, bad farming methods introduced by Europeans have led to the ruin of land. In tropical countries, rainforest is being cut down by logging companies and scientists think that this may harm the atmosphere. In 1992, a conference called the Rio Summit took place in Rio de Janeiro, Brazil, which caused governments to promise to help the environment.

See above pages for more information.

A bulldozer clearing space in the Amazon rainforest. It is making way for oil exploration.

☐ Main areas of rainforest
☐ Rainforest in severe danger

Areas where rainforest grows and where it is being cut down.

Rainforest trees are also cut down for timber and to make room for farming and road building.

THE 20TH CENTURY ENDS

During the Cold War, communism was a major force in Europe and the world. In the 1980s, communist governments in Eastern Europe fell from power breathtakingly quickly. Before long, the Soviet Union had broken up as well. The closing years of the 20th century began to see great changes in the balance of world power.

The symbol of the Polish trade union, Solidarity.

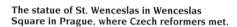
The statue of St. Wenceslas in Wenceslas Square in Prague, where Czech reformers met.

SOLIDARITY IN POLAND

The rise against communism began in Poland. The Polish people were not happy that the Soviet Union dominated their government. In 1980, the non-communist trade union, called Solidarity, and the Catholic Church made an alliance. They forced the government to give them more rights, such as the right to free elections and freedom of speech.

The authorities tried to restore their power by introducing martial law (when the armed forces took control) and by banning Solidarity. Solidarity's campaign grew, however, and in 1989 the Polish people were granted free elections. In 1990, the communists were voted out.

THE IRON CURTAIN DISSOLVES

Events in Poland led other countries to change. In Hungary, Bulgaria and Czechoslovakia, the communists allowed new political parties. Only in Romania did the old government try to cling to power, leading to a bloody struggle. Hungary then opened its borders to Austria in 1989.

The Iron Curtain which had divided Europe for nearly 50 years had dissolved. The streets of Leipzig and Berlin in East Germany were filled with people demanding change. In November 1989, East Germany's new leader agreed that the Berlin Wall should be dismantled. Within seven months, Germany was reunited.

Border changes followed the revolts against communism. Germany was reunited and Czechoslovakia separated into two.

THE END OF THE SOVIET UNION

In 1985, the Soviet President Gorbachev launched a series of reforms, called *Perestroika* ("restructuring"). They were intended to modernize the Soviet Union, but in the turmoil the ties between its individual republics became weak. By 1989, every republic had a new system of political parties. Eventually Gorbachev had to agree to break up the Soviet Union.

The traditional communists were outraged and tried to take over. They failed, but Gorbachev lost power. On December 31, 1991, the Soviet Union was broken up. Fighting then broke out in many of the new states as rival groups struggled for power.

The former Soviet Republics, which are now independent states. Lithuania, Latvia and Estonia were the first to declare independence.

YUGOSLAVIA

When the leader of Yugoslavia, Marshall Tito, died in 1980, its states began to break away from each other. In 1991, Slovenia and Croatia declared independence. Serbia used armed forces to try to stop them and civil war broke out. The war then spread to Bosnia and Herzegovina. The war here grew much worse and the United Nations failed to stop it.

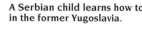
A Serbian child learns how to use a gun in the former Yugoslavia.

The former Yugoslavia. Slovenia, Croatia and Serbia are now separate. Serbs, Croats and Bosnians fight over Bosnia and Herzegovina.

DEMOCRACY IN CHINA

Calls for free elections also grew in China, the world's biggest communist power. In April 1989, around 100,000 students marched through the streets of the capital Beijing and occupied the main public area, Tiananmen Square. The army, which was loyal to the government, moved in to break up the crowd of protesters.

In the following confrontation, thousands were killed in Beijing itself and also across China. The communist government ignored protests from other countries and stood firm against those calling for greater democracy.

Students protest in Beijing's Tiananmen Square, gathering around a replica of the Statue of Liberty.

ISLAM – A WORLD FORCE

In the early 1980s, an old force began to gain power – Islam. The dispute between the Israelis and Palestinians in the Middle East was seen as a religious struggle. Enthusiasm for Islam in Arab countries grew.

The focus of this was Iran, where a revolution had taken place in 1979. The new leaders were religious officials called *ayatollahs*, who insisted on Islamic law. It became clear, though, that the Arab world was not united when Iraq invaded Iran in 1980. A terrible war followed, and fighting did not stop until 1988. In 1990, Iraq then invaded Kuwait, resulting in the Gulf War. An attack by the United Nations led to a swift defeat for Iraq.

In the Gulf War, United Nations forces included troops from the USA, the Soviet Union, Europe, Saudi Arabia and other Arab nations.

SOUTH AFRICA

South Africa suffered great problems during the late 20th century. World opinion denounced its system of apartheid, which denied rights to nonwhite people. Many nations refused to have contact with it. By 1990, President F. W. de Klerk realized that the way forward was to end apartheid.

Doing this was not easy. Some whites reacted against this change. Also the two main black political parties, the African National Congress and the Zulu Inkatha Party, fought for power. In 1994, however, South Africa held free elections. Nelson Mandela, the leader of the ANC, became the country's first black president.

South Africans wait to vote in the 1994 elections. The banner inviting people to vote is written in four languages – English, Afrikaans, Sotho and Nguni.

WORLD TIME CHART

This chart shows events in each continent from pre-history to the present day.

DATE	AFRICA	AMERICAS	ASIA	AUSTRALASIA	EUROPE
EARLY TIMES	Most scientists think that humans first evolved from apes around 2.5 million years ago in Africa, and spread from there around the world.			Aboriginal people settle in Australia. Around 38,000 years ago they either sailed by canoe or walked across from Malaysia, which was then a bridge of land between Asia and Australia. No recorded history survives in this continent until later ages.	
9000BC		**c.9000BC** Having crossed from Asia to Alaska by land bridges, hunters are spreading south through America	**c.9000-8000BC** Animal and crop farming begins in the Fertile Crescent. **c.8000BC** Jericho flourishes in the Middle East.		**c.6500BC** Farming begins in Greece.
6000BC	**c.6000BC** Earliest rock paintings in the Saharan mountains.	**c.6000BC** Farming begins in Central America.	**c.6000BC** Çatal Hüyük flourishes in Asia Minor, producing the first known pottery and cloth made of wool.		**c.5500BC** Villages of mudbrick homes built in Greece and Bulgaria. Painted pottery made.
5000BC	**c.5000BC** Farming begins in Egypt.		**c.5000BC** People in Mesopotamia irrigate their crops. Bronze casting begins in Asia Minor.	**c.5000BC** Aboriginal settlements spread inland as sea levels rise.	
4000BC	**c.4000BC** Copper begins to be used in Egypt. **c.3500BC** Sails are used on ships in Egypt. **c.3200BC** Hieroglyphics appear in Egypt. Bronze is used. **c.3100BC** King Menes unites Upper and Lower Egypt.		**c.3500BC** The wheel is invented in Mesopotamia.		**c.3500BC** Stone tombs and circles are built in Brittany, Spain and Britain. **c.3250BC** Wheeled vehicles spread to Europe from Asia.
3000BC	**c.3000BC** Farming spreads to central Africa. **c.2590BC** Cheops builds the Great Pyramid at Giza in Egypt.	**c.3000BC** The first known pottery in America is made in Colombia and Equador.	**c.3000BC** Major cities develop in Sumer, and pictograms are invented. Bronze is used in Thailand. **c.2550BC** Civilizations grow in the Indus Valley. **c.2500BC** People from central Asia tame and use horses.		**c.3000BC** Copper working spreads across Europe. **c.3000-1500BC** Forests cleared and land is farmed in north and west Europe. Mining for flints.
2000BC	**c.2000BC** The Sahara becomes a desert as a result of climatic change. **c.1168BC** Rameses III, the last great Egyptian pharaoh, dies. **c.1000BC** Herders and early farmers spread south from Ethiopia into central Kenya and northern Tanzania.	**c.2000BC** The first metal working in America begins in Peru. **c.2000-1500BC** Pottery spreads among farmers in Peru. **c.1150BC** The beginning of the Olmec civilization in Mexico.	**c.1600BC** Shang Bronze Age culture thrives in China. **c.1500BC** Chinese script is invented. **c.1200BC** Beginning of Judaism. Jews are sent out of Egypt and settle in Palestine. **c.1100BC** Phoenicians spread into lands surrounding the Mediterranean Sea and develop an alphabetic script. **c.650BC** Iron Age begins in China.	**c.2000BC** People sail from Indonesia and begin to settle on the Pacific islands.	**c.2000BC** Greeks use sails on sea-going ships. **c.1600-1200BC** Mycenean civilization flourishes in Greece. **776BC** First recorded Olympic Games are held in Greece. **753BC** Rome is founded, according to legend.
500BC	**c.500BC** Iron working spreads through the south Sahara.		**c.480BC** Siddhartha Gautama, founder of Buddhism, dies.		**c.500BC** Celtic art emerges in northern Europe. **479-338BC** Greek Classical culture flourishes.

DATE	AFRICA	AMERICAS	ASIA	AUSTRALASIA	EUROPE
300BC		**c.300BC** Rise of Zapotec culture in Mexico. Decline of Olmec civilisation. **c.200BC-AD700** Rise of Teotihuacan culture in Mexico.	**c.300BC** The stirrup is invented in central Asia. Fighting on horseback is easier. **202BC** China is united by the Han Dynasty. **c.112BC** The Silk Road opens between China and the Middle East.	Aboriginal people in Australia continue to thrive by skilled hunting and gathering, although no records survive of historical events. A rich artistic and spiritual culture develops, known as the Dreaming.	**264-241BC** Rome and Carthage fight in the First Punic War. **218-201BC** Second Punic War.
100BC	**c.100BC** Camels brought to the Sahara from the Middle East and north Africa. **30BC** Cleopatra, the Egyptian queen, dies and Egypt becomes a Roman province.	**c.100BC** Hohokam people in North America irrigate fields with ditches and dykes.	**c.100BC** North India invaded by Greeks and nomadic tribes including the Kushans.		**73-71BC** Spartacus, a slave, leads an unsuccessful slave revolt in Rome.
0	**c.AD50** Kingdom of Axum (Ethiopia) begins to expand. **c.AD70** Christianity reaches Alexandria in Egypt, and spreads slowly south. **c.AD400** Axum leaders have converted to Christianity. **AD429** Vandals set up a kingdom in north Africa.	**c.AD250** The Mayans of central America adopt hieroglyphic alphabet. **c.AD300** Hopewell Indians in North America flourish. The Maya flourish in central America. **c.AD500-1200** Totonac culture in Mexico flourishes, building stepped pyramids.	**c.0** Birth of Jesus Christ. **c.AD30** Jesus Christ, founder of Christianity, is crucified in Jerusalem. **c.AD105** Paper is invented in China. **AD132** Jews rebel against the Romans and are forced to leave Palestine. **AD320** Gupta Empire is founded in India. **AD400-500** First Sanskrit writing in Cambodia, Java and Borneo. **c.AD520** A decimal mathematics system is invented in India.		**AD117** Roman Empire is at its greatest extent. **AD313** Christianity is tolerated in the Roman Empire. **AD330** Constantinople becomes the capital of the Roman Empire. **AD410** Visigoths invade Italy and sack Rome. **AD486** The Kingdom of the Franks is founded in modern day France and Germany.
AD600	**AD611-14** Persians take Jerusalem from Byzantines. **AD641** Arabs conquer Egypt and begin their conquest of north Africa.	**c.AD600** The Maya Empire is at its peak. Astronomers predict eclipses and calculate the solar year. **c.AD600-1000** The northwest coast of South America is populated by many flourishing independent states.	**AD624** T'ang Dynasty begin to rule in China. **AD632** Muhammad, founder of Islam, dies.		**c.AD610** The Eastern Roman Empire becomes influenced by Greek culture and becomes known as the Byzantine Empire.
AD700	**c.AD700-1200** Empire of Ghana flourishes in west Africa. The Kingdom of Axum in Ethiopia is in conflict with the rising power of Islam.	**AD750** Teotihuacan is destroyed. Mayan civilization slowly declines.	**c.AD730** Wooden block printing is invented in China.		**AD711** Muslims from Africa, called the Moors, invade Spain. **c.AD790** Vikings make the first raids on Britain.
AD800	**c.AD800-1800** Kingdom of Kanem Bornu thrives in west Africa.	**AD850** The great Nahua invasion from north Mexico begins. The Toltec tribe found Tula.	**AD853** The first printed book is made in China.	**c.AD800** Ancestors of the Maoris arrive on New Zealand from other Pacific islands. Easter Island is also settled at this time.	**AD800** Charlemagne, King of the Franks, is crowned Emperor of the Romans by the Pope. **AD850** Viking raids on Europe are at a peak. **AD882** Kiev becomes the capital of Russia.

WORLD TIME CHART

DATE	AFRICA	AMERICAS	ASIA	AUSTRALASIA	EUROPE
900					
	AD969 Fatimids from eastern north Africa conquer Egypt and found Cairo.	**c.AD990** The Inca Empire in South America grows.	**AD979** The Sung Dynasty begin its rule in China.		**AD911** Vikings take control of Normandy in France.
1000	**c.1000**			**c.1000**	
	The first iron age settlement is founded at Zimbabwe in southern Africa. **1052** Almoravids attack Ghana and go on to rule a kingdom in north Africa and Spain.	**c.1002** The Vikings colonize Greenland and visit the North American mainland.	**c.1045** Printing with movable type is invented in China. **1071** The Byzantine Empire is defeated by Seljuk Turks at the Battle of Manzikert. **1096** The First Crusade leaves Europe for the Middle East.	In New Zealand Maori people live by cultivating crops such as sweet potato, and catch fish and birds. By now they have built settlements on rivers, bays and lagoons in Hawke's Bay and are exploring the South Island.	**1054** The Christian Church splits into Orthodox and Catholic Churches in the Great Schism. **1066** Norman Conquest of Britain – French Duke William of Normandy becomes King of England.
1100	**c.1100**	**c.1100**			**c.1100**
	Growth of the kingdom of Ife in Nigeria. **c.1150** Islam is flourishing in north Africa.	The Toltecs flourish in Mexico.	**1126** The Ch'in Dynasty conquer northern China. **1175** The first Muslim Empire is founded in India. **1188** Saladin destroys the Crusader States in the Middle East.		The first European universities are founded. **1153** Henry II comes to the English throne, beginning the Angevin Empire in England and France.
1200	**c.1200**	**c.1200**			
	The Mali Empire flourishes in west Africa. **c.1250** Berber states in north Africa become so powerful that Europe calls the area "the Barbary Coast".	The Aztecs flourish in Mexico. **c.1250** The Aztecs build their capital Tenochtitlan.	**1206** Genghis Khan begins the Mongol conquest of Asia. **1234** Mongols destroy the Ch'in Empire in China. **1264** The Mongol ruler Kublai Khan founds the Yuan Dynasty in China.		**1233** Pope Gregory IX establishes the Inquisition to suppress heresy. **1239** The Mongols conquer Russia. **c.1290** Spectacles are invented in Italy.
1300	**c.1300**	**c.1300**			
	The Benin Empire emerges in west Africa.	Inca civilization is emerging in present-day Peru. Manco Capac, the Inca leader, founds Cuzco as the capital city.	**1368** The Ming Dynasty is founded in China. **1380** Mongol leader Tamerlane is building his empire in Asia.		**1339-1453** France and Britain fight in the Hundred Years' War.
1400				**c.1400**	
	1415 The Portuguese make the first European conquest in Africa at Ceuta in Morocco. **c.1430** Great stone buildings are erected at Zimbabwe. **c.1450** The Songhai Empire flourishes in west Africa. **1471-82** The Portuguese conquer and settle parts of north and east Africa. **1492** The Spaniards begin to conquer north Africa. **1493** The Songhai Empire in west Africa reaches its peak.	**c.1427** The Aztecs are growing increasingly powerful and aggressive. Emperor Itzcoatl forces other tribes to pay tributes. **c.1440** A new aqueduct brings fresh water from Chapultec spring into the city of Tenochtitlan. **1492** Columbus reaches the Caribbean, the first European to land in the Americas. **1494** The Spaniards settle on Hispaniola. The Treaty of Tordesillas divides the undiscovered world between the Spaniards and the Portuguese.	**1421** Beijing becomes the capital of China. **1447** Provinces in India, Persia and Afghanistan win independence from Tamerlane's empire. **1477** Provincial wars erupt between daimyos, local barons in Japan. **1494** Babur, descendant of Genghis Khan, becomes Prince of Ferghana, central Asia. **1497** Vasco da Gama becomes the first European to sail to India and back.	Climatic changes make life much harder for the hunter-gatherers of Australasia. "The Little Ice Age" forces Maoris on New Zealand to become more nomadic as their food supplies become less plentiful. Exploring inland regions, they discover *pounamu*, a kind of jade which is harder than steel. This improves their tools and technology.	**1429** Joan of Arc leads French troops to victory against the English, but is burned at the stake in 1431. **1453** Gutenberg invents first European printing press. Ottoman Turks take Constantinople, ending the Byzantine Empire. **1478** Ivan III throws off the Mongol rule in Russia. **1492** Granada, the last Moorish stronghold in Spain, is reconquered by the Spanish. A royal command forces Jews to leave Spain as a renewal of the Inquisition.

WORLD TIME CHART

DATE	AFRICA	AMERICAS	ASIA	AUSTRALASIA	EUROPE
1500			**1500**		**c.1500**
	1505 The Portuguese set up trading posts in east Africa. **1517** Turks conquer Egypt. **c.1520** People from coastal regions of western Africa begin to be taken by force to the Americas to work on slave estates. **1562** John Hawkins makes the first British slave trade voyage, taking slaves from west Africa to the Caribbean.	**1519-22** Cortes conquers the Aztecs. **c.1520** African slaves begin to be taken to America. **1531-34** Pizarro conquers the Incas. **1541** Indians revolt in Mexico against the Spanish. **1542** Charles V abolishes Indian slavery in the Spanish colonies. As a result, the use of African slaves increases. **1584** Walter Raleigh founds an English colony in Virginia, which does not survive.	The Safavid Dynasty is founded in Persia. **1520-66** Reign of Suleiman the Magnificent. The Ottoman Empire reaches its peak. **1526** Babur conquers the Kingdom of Delhi and founds the Mogul Empire in India. **1570** Japan opens Nagasaki to foreign traders. **1581** Russians take Siberia.	Aboriginal and Maori culture continues to develop and thrive, until the arrival of the Europeans.	The Italian Renaissance is at its peak. **1517** Martin Luther begins to protest against the Catholic Church, starting the Reformation. **c.1525** The potato is brought to Europe from South America. **1543** Nicholas Copernicus publishes his theories on the Solar System. **1559** Tobacco is brought to Europe from North America. **1571** Ottoman power in the Mediterranean ends at the Battle of Lepanto.
1600	**c.1600** The Oyo Kingdom in central west Africa reaches its peak. **1616** The Dutch and French explore west Africa and set up trading posts in Senegal and the Gold Coast. **1652** The Dutch found Cape Colony in southern Africa. **1659** The French found a trading post in Senegal.	**1607** The first permanent English settlement is founded at Jamestown, Virginia in North America. **1608** The French found Quebec in Canada. **1625** The Dutch found New Amsterdam. **1630-42** Seeking religious freedom, 16,000 English Puritans settle in Massachusetts Bay Colony on northeast coast of America. **1667** New Amsterdam becomes British and is renamed New York.	**c.1600** The Shogun rulers are at the height of power in Japan. **1619** The Dutch found their colony of Batavia in Indonesia. **1644** The Manchu Dynasty begin their rule in China. **1649** Russians reach the Pacific Ocean.	**1614-36** Europeans begin to explore the coast of Australia. **1642-43** Dutchman Tasman discovers Tasmania, New Zealand and Fiji. He explores the north and west coasts of Australia.	**1604** Peace between Spain and England after fighting since 1587 over religious differences and power at sea. **1618-48** The Thirty Years' War ravages Germany and Bohemia. **1658** Swedish Empire is at its peak. **c.1660** The great period of French culture is at its peak.
1700	**c.1700** The Asante Kingdom in west Africa is at its peak as the Yoruba Kingdom in the same area is in decline. The Bantu Kingdom in east Africa is rising. **1750** The slave trade is at its peak. **1775** The Masai expand in east Africa, reaching the Ngong Hills. **1798-99** Napoleon invades Egypt. He is defeated by the British, but defeats the Turks in a separate battle.	**1728** Bering begins the Russian exploration of Alaska **1759-60** Britain wins territory in Canada from the French. **1775-83** American War of Independence. **1776** American Declaration of Independence. The United States of America is founded. **1789** George Washington becomes the first President of the United States.	**1715** China conquers Mongolia and East Turkestan. **1761** The British gain control of India from the French. **1775-82** The British fight the Marathas princes in India. **1782** Rama I is crowned King of Siam (later Thailand), the only Southeast Asian country to remain uncolonized. **1787** Severe famine and rice riots in Edo, Japan.	**1721-22** Dutchman Roggeveen finds Samoa, the Solomon Islands, and Easter Island. **1768-71** Englishman Cook explores the Pacific Ocean. **1770** Cook is the first European to land in Australia, known as New Holland. He claims it for Britain and renames it New South Wales. **1779** Cook is killed in Hawaii after becoming involved in a dispute. **1788** Convicts are transported from Britain to Sydney – the first permanent colony in Australia.	**1703** Peter the Great founds a new Russian capital – St. Petersburg. **1756-1791** Life of Wolfgang Amadeus Mozart, Austrian composer. **c.1770** New ideas on science and technology start the Industrial Revolution. **c.1780** European campaign against slavery gathers pace. **1789-92** The French Revolution.

WORLD TIME CHART

DATE	AFRICA	AMERICAS	ASIA	AUSTRALASIA	EUROPE
1800			**1800**		
	1818 The Zulu Kingdom is founded in southern Africa.	**1808-28** South and central American states including Chile, Mexico and Brazil, gain independence from Spain and Portugal.	Britain starts to import opium into China, leading eventually to the Opium Wars in 1839.	**1804** Hobart, in Tasmania, is founded. **c.1820** In Australia, settlers begin to move inland from coastal towns.	**1804** Napoleon Bonaparte becomes Emperor of the French. **1815** Napoleon is finally defeated at the Battle of Waterloo and is exiled to St. Helena.
	1822 Liberia is founded as a colony for freed slaves from America. **1830** The French conquer Algiers and start to colonize Algeria. **1835-37** The start of the Great Trek of Boers (Dutch settlers in south Africa) from the Cape to find new lands to settle. **1838-39** The Boers defeat the Zulus and found the Republic of Natal. **1844** War between France and Morocco.	**1826** President Monroe warns Europeans not to interfere with American politics. **1830s** American settlers move west. **1836** Texas breaks free of Mexican rule. It later becomes an American state. **1840-41** Upper and Lower Canada are united. Britain grants the province self-government, though it remains under the Crown.	**1833** The British East India Company trade monopoly with India and China is ended. **1839-42** Britain and China fight in the First Opium War. **1843-49** British extend power in India to include Sind and Punjab.	**1826** Settlers and Aborigines fight the Black War in Tasmania. **1840** Britain annexes New Zealand as part of its empire. Maori chiefs are forced to submit to British rule. **1844-45** Stuart explores central Australia.	**1822** First photograph is produced in France. **1825** First passenger railway is opened in Britain. **1833** Slavery is abolished in the British Empire. **1839** The six English Tolpuddle Martyrs are sent to Australia as a punishment for forming a trade union. **1845-48** The Irish Great Famine leads to mass emigration to USA.
	1853 Scottish missionary David Livingstone begins to explore Africa.	**1846-48** The USA and Mexico are at war. **1848** Gold is found in California. **1859** Oil is discovered in Pennsylvania.	**1853** Japan is forced by US gunboats to open its ports after a long period of isolation. **1857-58** The Indian Mutiny against British rule. Moguls deposed. **1860** The Second Opium War ends.	**1844-48** Maori uprisings against the British fail in New Zealand. **1853-54** A gold rush breaks out in Victoria, Australia as gold mines are discovered. **1860-61** Explorers Burke and Wills cross Australia.	**1848** A wave of revolutions sweeps across Europe. Marx publishes Communist Manifesto. **1853-56** Britain and Russia fight in the Crimean War.
	1860 French begin expansion in west Africa. **1867** Diamonds discovered in Boer territory. **1869** Suez Canal opens. **1877-1914** Colonial powers speed up "the scramble for Africa". **1899-1902** The Boer War. Britain eventually defeats the Boers in southern Africa.	**1861-65** American Civil War. Slavery is abolished and the South loses the war. **1867** Canada achieves greater self-rule within the British Empire. **1869** The first railway crosses America. **1890** Battle of Wounded Knee – the last American Indian battle with the US Army.	**1862-1908** Empress Tz'u-hsi rules China. **1864** The Taiping Rebellion in China against the decaying Manchu Dynasty. **1868** Emperors are restored to power in Japan with the decline of the military Shogun leaders, who had ruled for 670 years.	**1860-64** New Zealand and Britain fight Maori Wars. **1863** Gold rush in New Zealand. **1868** End of British transportation of convicts to Australia. **1872** Australia's overland telegraph completed. **1893** Women in New Zealand are the first to achieve the right to vote.	**1861** Italy achieves unification. Tsar Alexander II of Russia gives greater freedom to the serfs. **1865** Louis Pasteur, a French chemist, discovers bacteria. **1871** Germany achieves unification. **1885-90** Daimler and Benz develop the first cars in Germany. **1898** Marie Curie isolates radium.
1900	**c.1900** Copper mining starts in the Congo in central Africa.	**1903** The first powered flight is achieved by the American Wright brothers at Kittyhawk.	**1900** Boxer Uprising against foreigners ends in China. **1904-05** Russia and Japan are at war.	**1901** States of Australia are united to make one country within the British Empire. **c.1905-30s** New Zealand benefits from refrigerated shipping and trade with Britain.	**1901** Death of Victoria, Queen of England. **1902-07** Britain makes alliances with Japan, France and Russia.
	1910 Union of South Africa is established as a self-governing British dominion. **1918** The Ottoman Empire collapses. **1919** Nationalist uprising in Egypt.	**1911** The Mexican Revolution. **1914** Panama Canal opens. **1917** USA joins the Allies in World War One. **c.1920** Jazz music emerges in the USA.	**1911** China becomes a republic after the Chinese Revolution. **1917** "Balfour Declaration" promises Jews a homeland in Palestine. **1922** Reign of the last Ottoman Sultan ends. A republic is set up in Turkey.	**1907** New Zealand achieves greater self-rule as a dominion in the British Empire. **1919** Smith brothers make first flight from Australia to Britain. **1927** Canberra becomes the capital of Australia.	**1910** Revolution in Portugal. **1914-18** World War One. **1917** The Russian Revolution. **1919** The League of Nations is established. **1922** Mussolini comes to power in Italy.

WORLD TIME CHART

DATE	AFRICA	AMERICAS	ASIA	AUSTRALASIA	EUROPE
1920				**c.1920**	
	1925 Moroccan rebellion against French rule.	**1927** In the USA, the first "talkies", movies with a spoken soundtrack, appear.	**1921** Mao Zedong forms the Chinese Communist Party.	Australia and New Zealand's trade with Britain grows. Britain helps people migrate to Australia and New Zealand.	**1926** John Logie Baird develops the television.
	1920s Lebanon, Syria and Iraq achieve independence from French and British rule.	**1929** World depression begins with the Wall Street Crash (fall of US Stock Market).	**1929** Gandhi calls for Indian independence.		**1933** Hitler's Nazi party takes power in Germany.
	1930 Ethiopia is ruled by Emperor Haile Selassie.		**1937** China and Japan are at war.	**1933** Samoans protest against New Zealand rule.	**1936-39** Spanish Civil War, won by Fascists.
	1935 Italy invades Ethiopia.	**1941** USA joins the Allies in World War Two.	**1941** Japan attacks Pearl Harbor in the USA, bringing it into World War Two.	**1939-45** Australian and New Zealand troops fight alongside Allied army in north Africa and Italy. They counter Japanese threats to East Indies (Indonesia), Papua and the Philippines.	**1939-45** World War Two.
	1940-43 World War Two in Africa – Axis Powers eventually lose struggle in Egypt, and Italy is driven out of Ethiopia and surrounding area.	**1942-45** Nuclear technology develops in the USA.			**1945** The Cold War between Soviet Union and the USA begins.
		1945 The United Nations is formed.	**1945** The USA ends war in the Pacific when it drops two atomic bombs on Japan.		**1946** War trials of Nazi leaders in Nuremberg, Germany.
		1947 USA announces the Marshall Plan giving aid to Europe. Juan Peron becomes President of Argentina, backed by the army. Much of South America is now ruled by military dictators until mid 80s. Exceptions include Cuba under communist leader Castro (1958-present) and Chile briefly under Allende (1970-73).	**1947** India and Pakistan become independent.		**1948** Communists take over in Czechoslovakia, Romania, Bulgaria, Poland and Hungary.
			1948 The state of Israel is formed. The first Arab-Israeli War erupts.		
	1949 South African government introduces apartheid, which deprives nonwhite people of their rights and liberty.		**1949** Communists take power in China.	**c.1949-52** Mass immigration of people displaced by war.	**1953-56** Anti-communist risings in Eastern Europe.
			1950-53 The Korean War.	**c.1950** Australia and New Zealand shift toward USA in trade, alliances and culture.	**1957** EEC (Common Market) boosts trade in western Europe.
	1957 The Gold Coast becomes independent from Britain and is renamed Ghana.		**1957** Unsuccessful uprising in Tibet against China.	**1956** Television first broadcast in Australia.	
	c.1960 Many African nations become independent from their European colonizers.	**1958-67** US black people demand civil rights.	**1964-74** The Vietnam War.	**1964-72** New Zealand and Australia fight alongside USA in Vietnam.	**1961** The Berlin Wall is built. Uri Gagarin from the Soviet Union is the first man in space.
		c.1960 Rock and Roll begins in the USA.	**1975-79** The Khmer Rouge murder millions in Cambodia.	**1975** Papua New Guinea becomes independent of Australia.	**1977** Democracy restored in Spain after General Franco's death.
	1976 South Africa crushes Soweto riots.	**1969** US astronaut Neil Armstrong walks on the Moon. Demonstrations against Vietnam war.	**1979** Shah of Iran is deposed. An Islamic republic is set up.		
1980	**1980**	**c.1980**		**c.1980s**	**1980**
	Black majority rule is set up in Rhodesia, which is renamed Zimbabwe.	Computers spread throughout the west from the USA.	**1980-88** The Iran-Iraq War.	Australian and New Zealand trade turns increasingly to Japan as European internal market grows.	Polish trade union Solidarity challenges communist rule.
	1984 Famine strikes south of the Sahara.	**1982** Argentina invades Falkland Islands but is driven out by Britain.	**1983** Civil unrest between Tamils and Singhalese in Sri Lanka.		**1981** Widespread demonstrations against nuclear weapons in Europe.
	1985 South Africa suspends civil rights after unrest among black people.	**1983-85** Military governments lose power, and democracy is restored in Argentina, Brazil and Uruguay.	**1984** Assassination of Indian Prime Minister Indira Gandhi. Britain and China negotiate over Hong Kong.		**1985** Mikhail Gorbachev becomes leader of the USSR, and sets in motion *Perestroika* ("restructuring") reforms.
	1986 USA bombs Libya in retaliation against terrorist activities.	**1987** USA signs arms reduction treaty with the Soviet Union.	**1988** Palestinian *intifada* or uprising against Israeli occupation.		**1986** Explosion at Chernobyl nuclear power station in the Soviet Union.
	1989 UN supervises Namibian independence from South Africa.		**1989** Student democracy movement crushed in China. After 10 years Soviet troops leave Afghanistan.	**1990s** Growing desire in Australia to reduce links with British monarchy.	**1989** Communist governments fall in Eastern Europe. East and West Germany are united (1990).
	1990 South African government begins to dismantle apartheid.	**1990-91** Cold War ends as USA and Soviet Union join as allies against Iraq in the Gulf War.	**1990-91** Iraq beaten by United Nations forces in the Gulf War.		**1991** Soviet Union breaks up into independent states. Civil war breaks out in the former Yugoslavia.
	1994 Nelson Mandela becomes President of South Africa. Apartheid ends. Sanctions cease.	**1992** World leaders meet to discuss global environmental concerns at Rio Summit in Brazil.	**1993** Peace process underway between Israel and Palestinians..	**1995** People protest against France's plans to renew nuclear testing in the Pacific.	**1994** British-Irish peace talks over Ulster's future.

GLOSSARY

Below is a list of important words used in this book. Words printed in **bold** type within a definition have their own separate entry.

abdication A decision by the king or queen, or a prince in waiting, to give up his or her claim to the throne.

aid Money given by a country or organization to support poor or disaster-stricken areas.

ally An individual, group or country which gives help and support. An alliance is where allies agree to support one another.

apartheid The South African policy of keeping the different races apart, and depriving nonwhite people of their rights and liberty. The system of apartheid was finally dismantled by F. W. de Klerk and Nelson Mandela's new majority government.

archeology The study of history by digging up and examining remains.

assassination Murder, usually of someone famous or politically important.

Axis powers The countries allied to Germany in the Second World War – Italy, Japan, Hungary and others.

barbarians The name given by the Ancient Greeks to people they considered less civilized than themselves. The word was also used to describe the mainly Germanic tribes who undermined the Roman Empire. It is now used for any group of violent or uncivilized people.

Buddhism Buddhists believe in reincarnation (rebirth in another form). Buddhism is not based on the worship of any god or gods, but rather on finding the path to *nirvana* (peace or enlightenment) through meditation. The Buddha lived in India in the 6th century AD.

Catholicism The branch of **Christianity** based on the Pope's leadership from Rome. Catholics regard the Virgin Mary as a mediator between God and human beings.

Christianity The faith based on the teachings of Jesus Christ, set out in the New Testament. Christians believe Jesus is the son of God.

city-state A self-ruling city and its surrounding area, for instance ancient Athens.

civil war Fighting between rival groups or civilians within the same country.

civilization A group of people which has reached a high level of social and cultural development, for instance using a written language, or sophisticated arts, sciences and methods of government.

classical Relating to ancient Greek or Roman **civilization**, and also 17th and 18th century European culture that was based on it.

cold war A struggle for power by all means short of fighting. The term is usually used to describe the struggle for supremacy in the 1960s between the **superpowers,** the USA and the Soviet Union.

colony An area and its people ruled from another country. For instance, Nigeria was a British colony until its **independence** in 1960.

communism A political system based on Karl Marx's writings, where the state owns all land and factories, and provides for people's needs. In the late 1980s, many countries in Eastern Europe rejected communism.

crusade A military expedition or "holy war", usually used to describe **Christian** wars against **Muslim** forces from the 11th to 13th centuries.

culture The shared ideas, beliefs and values of a group of people.

democracy A system of government where every adult can vote to elect representatives in the Parliament or other governing body. There may be a **monarch**, but he or she has little real constitutional power. In Britain, for instance, Queen Elizabeth is head of state but has little influence over the elected government.

depose To remove someone (for instance a **dictator**) from power.

developing countries Nations, mostly in the southern hemisphere, which have not yet developed their full economic or industrial potential, often as a result of slavery or colonialism.

diaspora The dispersion of Jews across the world after they were forced to leave Palestine in the 1st century AD. The word is also now used for other groups who are dispersed from their homeland.

dictator A ruler whose word is law, imposed by military force.

dynasty A series of powerful leaders from the same family, for instance the pharaohs.

economy The financial structure made up of all goods and services produced, sold and bought in a country or region.

election When people vote to place a person or party in a position of power.

embargo A government order not to trade with another country.

empire A large area of land, and its people, ruled by one powerful person or government. Two examples are the Roman Empire, or the British Empire, which was at its height under Queen Victoria.

the Enlightenment The new freedom of thought in the 18th century, originating in France, which valued reason and human progress, tolerance of different religions, and a questioning of tradition and authority. Rulers like Catherine the Great of Russia were called "Enlightened Despots" because they retained absolute power but tried to improve the lives of their subjects.

equator An imaginary line encircling the Earth at an equal distance from the North and South Poles.

evolution The theory, first proposed by Charles Darwin, of how life on Earth gradually developed.

fascism The military form of government in Italy 1922-43, led by the **dictator** Benito Mussolini, which was driven by **nationalism** and hostility to **communism**. The Fascist government persecuted Jews, liberals and other groups, and restricted ordinary people's freedom. The name is also used for people or parties with similar views in other countries, such as Hitler's Germany.

feudalism The system in Europe in the **Middle Ages** where the **monarch** or overlord gave land to nobles in return for military support or money. **Serfs** farmed the nobles' land.

franchise The right to vote. After all men had gained the vote, **Suffragettes** in Britain and USA campaigned for women's vote.

guerilla war Where a small band of fighters combats a larger army. Guerilla fighters often fight for their strong political beliefs.

heretic Someone whose beliefs go against those of the established Church.

Hinduism The major faith in India. Hindus believe in reincarnation (rebirth in another form) and pray to many gods and goddesses. The Hindu caste system rigidly ranked groups in society according to their "purity" or importance, but the system is gradually losing its hold.

Holy Roman Empire A group of Germanic peoples under the power of an emperor, who claimed the God-given right to rule. Charlemagne formed the empire in about AD800, and it reached its height under Charles V early in the 16th century. After the Napoleonic Wars the empire was dissolved and Germany was divided up into many separate states.

Homo sapiens Early humans, who had developed the use of tools. *Homo sapiens* lived about 250,000 years ago.

hunter-gatherers People who get food by hunting animals and gathering roots and berries, rather than farming the land.

imperial Relating to the **empire** or its emperor or empress.

independence Self-rule, especially when it is achieved after a nation has been ruled by a foreign power.

Industrial Revolution The economic and social changes which swept across Europe in the late 18th and 19th centuries. From small, cottage industries, manufacturing shifted to giant mechanized factories and mills. There was a huge population shift into the new cities.

Islam The religion of **Muslims**. Islam is based on the Ko'ran, the holy book which sets out the word of Allah (God) as revealed to prophet Muhammad (AD570-632).

Judaism The religion of the Jews, based on worship of one God whose word is set down in the Torah (the first five books of the Old Testament). Jews do not worship Jesus, and believe the messiah has yet to come to save humankind.

Kaiser The German name for "Emperor". The word comes from the Latin, "Caesar" after Julius Caesar.

Medieval – see entry for **Middle Ages**.

mercenary A soldier who fights for any army, as long as he is paid.

Middle Ages (or Medieval period) The period of European history between about AD1050 and AD1450, the start of the **Renaissance**.

Middle East The Arabic-speaking region to the east of the Mediterranean Sea, along with Turkey, Cyprus, Iran and most of north Africa.

Moguls The followers or descendants of Babur, a **Mongol** prince. Babur conquered Delhi in 1526, establishing the Mogul **dynasty** which ruled India until the 18th century.

monarch The head of state (king or queen) who inherits the crown. Few monarchs now have real power, and government carries out the job of ruling .

Mongols The people of Mongolia in central Asia. In the 12th century, Genghis Khan created a Mongol **empire** which stretched across Asia and parts of the Middle East and Russia.

Muslim Someone who follows the faith of **Islam**.

nationalism The feeling of common bond among people who share a region, **culture**, language or religion. Nationalism leads people to strive for unity and self-government.

nazism The fascist National Socialist movement, led by Adolf Hitler in Germany. During World War Two, the Nazis created death camps like Auschwitz, where they murdered up to 12 million people – Jews, gypsies, homosexuals and political prisoners.

Neanderthal Early humans, living between one million to 200,000 years ago, who used basic tools. Remains of Neanderthal humans were first discovered in 1857 in Germany, and were named after the Neander Valley in which they were found.

New World The European term for North and South America, during the period in which this area was being **colonized**, from the 16th century onwards.

Orthodox Christianity At the Great Schism in AD1054, the Orthodox Church broke away from Roman **Catholic** tradition. Instead of the Pope it was led by the Patriarch from Constantinople, the heart of the Byzantine Empire. Icons (holy pictures richly painted with gold leaf) are a feature of Orthodox Christianity, which is growing in strength again in Russia and the Balkans after being suppressed under **communist** rule.

Protestantism The branch of **Christianity** which broke away from Roman **Catholicism** at the **Reformation** in the 16th century. Initiated by Martin Luther, Protestantism rejected the Pope's spiritual · leadership.

rainforest Broadleaved, evergreen tropical forest, with very heavy rainfall, rich in plant and animal life. Rainforests, which are mainly in the southern hemisphere, contribute to global production of oxygen. Many are under threat from development for commercial purposes.

Reformation The movement in 16th century Europe to reform the Roman **Catholic** Church, which led to the founding of **Protestantism.**

refugee Someone who has been forced to leave their country to find shelter in a safer place. Refugees have often fled from war or famine, or else from imprisonment or death threats for their religious or political beliefs.

Renaissance The revival of arts and science that marked the transition from the **Middle Ages** to the modern world. The word "renaissance" means rebirth.

republic A state where the people vote for their government in an **election**. A republic has no king or queen.

revolution The overthrow of **monarch** or government by mass action by the people.

serf Under **feudalism** (especially in Europe in the **Middle Ages**) a serf was a peasant who was not free to leave the land because he or she was bound to it. If the land were sold, the serf would be passed onto the new landlord. Serfdom was abolished in Russia only in 1861.

Shintoism The native religion of Japan. Shinto ("the Sacred Way") involves worship of the emperor and many gods, as well as ancestors and sacred mountains, trees and waterfalls.

shogun The commander-in-chief and real ruler of feudal Japan. The Shogunate was the state or the military government led by the Shogun.

Sikhism is based on the teachings of Guru Nanak. At their temple or *gurdwara*, Sikhs pray to one God and share food as a symbol of equality. All Sikhs share the surnames *Singh* for men and *Kaur* for women. Sikhs are campaigning for an independent homeland in northern India.

slave triangle The three-way trade in the 18th century. European traders brought goods to west Africa, and traded them for African people. These people were shipped in atrocious conditions to the Americas, where they were sold as slaves. The traders then sailed back to Europe carrying goods grown in the Americas like coffee, sugar and tobacco.

socialism A political system whereby every member of society has equal rights, all factories and farms are run by and for the people, and wealth is distributed fairly.

suffragettes Women who campaigned for suffrage (the right to vote) in Britain at the end of the 19th and the beginning of the 20th century. Suffragettes drew attention to their cause by getting arrested and going on hunger strike in prison.

superpower A very powerful state. The term is usually applied to the USA or the former Soviet Union.

treaty A formal agreement between countries, usually relating to peace, trade or becoming **allies**.

Tsar (or **czar**) The Russian name for "Emperor". The word is a Slavonic form of the Latin "Caesar".

MAP INDEX

This index lists all the place names shown on the maps. As well as page numbers, it gives the country or region for each place, and alternative names through history, for example: Edo (now Tokyo).

A

Abyssinia (now Ethiopia), east Africa 62
Acadia (former French territory), North America 41
Achaea Roman Empire 18
Acre Middle East 32
Aden Middle East 62
Adriatic Sea Italy 37, 66
Adwalton Moor *battle* England 44
Aegean Sea Greece 16, 17, 31
Afghanistan Asia 74
Africa 7, 38, 73
    ancient civilizations 8
    colonization 62, 64
    continent forms 4-5
    early African empires 25
    earnings per person 76
    first people 6-7
    independence and development 73, 76-77
    languages 12
    rainforest 77
    slave trade 50-51
Agincourt *battle* France 28
Alaska Russian territory 58
    USA 60
Albania southeastern Europe 65, 69, 70, 71, 74, 78
Alexandria Egypt 31
Algeria north Africa 70, 73
Algiers (now in Algeria), north Africa 30
America – see North America, South America or
    United States of America
Amiens France 66
Amoy China 49
Angola southern Africa 62
Antarctica 4, 5, 39
Antioch Middle East 32
Anyang China 9
Arabia 23, 31, 67
Arabian Sea 24
Aragon Spain 28
Aral Sea Asia 16
Arctic Ocean 46
Argentina South America 57
Armenia Asia Minor 78
Arras France 66
Asia 7, 34-35, 63
    ancient civilizations 8-9
    early empires in Asia 24
    earnings per person 76
    colonization 62-63, 64
    continent forms 5
    first people 6-7
    independence and development 72, 76
    languages 12
    rainforest 77
    religions 22-23
    trade 24, 55
Asia Minor 9, 30-31, 79
Assyria Asia 8
Athens Greece 16, 17
Atlantic Ocean 6, 50
    battles 43, 56, 67
    explorers' routes 27, 38
    shipping and trade routes 50-51, 55, 67
Austerlitz *battle* (now Slavkov), Czech Republic 56
Australia 4-5, 39
    continent forms 4, 5,
    earnings per person 76
    European exploration 39
    colonization 62, 63
    first people 6, 7
    rainforest 77
    trade 55
Austria 45, 69, 78
Austrian Empire 59, 65, 66
Avignon France 33
Ayas Asia Minor 35

B

Azerbaijan Asia Minor 78
Aztec Empire central America 40

Babylon Middle East 8, 14
Babylonia Middle East 8
Baghdad (now in Iraq), Middle East 27, 31, 34, 35
Baku (now in Azerbaijan), Asia Minor 35
Baltic Sea northern Europe 44, 47, 59, 66
Bandai Japan 52
Basutoland South Africa 64
Bechuanaland (now Botswana), southern Africa 62
Beijing China 49
Belarus Europe 78
Belfast Northern Ireland 70
Belgian Congo (now Zaire), central Africa 62
Belgium northern Europe 66, 69, 70, 78
Belgrade Serbia 31
Bengal, Bay of Indian Ocean 24
Bering Sea 46
Berlin Germany 70, 71, 74
Bhutan Asia 72
Biafra central Africa 77
Birmingham England 70
Biwa *lake* Japan 52
Black Sea Asia Minor 16, 30-31
Bolivia South America 57
Bologna Italy 28, 37
Bombay India 35
Bonampak Mexico 24
Borneo Southeast Asia 35
Borodino *battle* Russia 56
Bosnia-Herzegovina eastern Europe 59, 66, 78
Botswana southern Africa 73
Brandenburg (now part of Germany), central
    Europe 44
Brazil South America 50, 57
Bristol England 70
Britain northern Europe 20, 44, 68
    Angles and Saxons 20, 21
    British Empire 62-63
    Industrial Revolution 54-55
    Vikings 27
    World War Two 70
Britannia Roman Empire 18
British East Africa (now Kenya), eastern Africa 62,
    67
British Guiana South America 57, 62
British Honduras central America 57
Brunei Southeast Asia 63
Brusa Middle East 31
Bukavu Zaire 77
Bulgaria eastern Europe 28, 65, 69, 70, 71, 74
Burma Asia 63, 71, 72
Burundi central Africa 73
Byzantine Empire Europe/Asia Minor 21, 30

C

Cairo Egypt 31
Calais *battle* France 28
Cambodia Southeast Asia 63, 72, 74
Cambridge, England 28
Cameroon western Africa 62, 73, 77
Canaan Middle East 23
Canada North America 51, 60, 61, 74
Canton China 49
Cape Bojador northwestern Africa 38
Cape Colony South Africa 64
Cape of Good Hope South Africa 38
Cape Town South Africa 64
Cardiff Wales 70
Caribbean Sea 24, 41, 50, 51, 75
Carthage north Africa 18, 19
Caspian Sea Asia 16, 30, 79

Castile Spain 28
Castillon *battle* France 28
Çatal Hüyük Asia Minor 8
Central African Republic central Africa 73
Central America 40, 41, 57
    early civilizations 9, 24
    European exploration
    and colonization 40
    trade 50-51, 55
Ceylon (now Sri Lanka), south Asia 63, 72
Chad central Africa 73, 77
Chad *lake* central Africa 25
Chagatai Empire Asia 34
Chartres France 28
Chichén Itza Mexico 24
Chile South America 57
China Asia 48-49, 74
    Chinese explorers 38, 48
    dynasties 24, 34, 48-49
    earnings per head 76
    Japan, conflict with 53, 64
    Marco Polo's journey 35
    religion 22
    Shang civilization 9
Ciudad Roderigo *battle* Spain 56
Clermont France 32
Coba Maya Empire 24
Cologne Germany 28, 70
Colombia South America 57
Confederate States USA 61
Confederation of the Rhine Germany 56
Congo *river* Africa 25
Congo, The southern Africa 50, 73
Constantinople (now Istanbul), Asia Minor 20, 26,
    27, 31, 32
Copan Maya Empire 24
Coral Sea *battle* Pacific Ocean 71
Corinth Greece 16
Corsica *island* Mediterranean Sea 30, 69
Costa Rica central America 57
Coventry England 70
Crécy *battle* France 28
Creta (Crete) *island* Roman Empire 18
Crete *island* Mediterranean Sea 8, 16, 31, 37
Croatia, eastern Europe 78
Cuba *island* Caribbean Sea 50, 65
    European arrival 40
    missile crisis 75
Curaçao *islands* Caribbean Sea 41
Cuzco Peru 40
Cyprus *island* Mediterranean Sea 9, 14, 31, 32
Cyreniaica Roman Empire 18
Czech Republic eastern Europe 78
Czechoslovakia (now Czech Republic and Slovakia),
    eastern Euope 69, 70, 74

D

Dacia Roman Empire 18
Dahomey (now Benin), western Africa 73
Damascus Middle East 8, 31
Delhi India 35, 72
Delos *island* Aegean Sea 17
Denmark Scandinavia 42, 44, 69
    World War Two 70
Dhaka (now in Bangladesh), Asia 72
Dijon France 33
Djibouti eastern Africa 73
Dominican Republic *island* Caribbean Sea 65
Dresden Germany 70
Drogheda *battle* Ireland 44
Dublin *battle* Ireland 44
Dunbar *battle* Scotland 44
Dunkirk *battle* France 70
Durham England 28
Dutch Borneo Southeast Asia 63
Dutch East Indies (now Indonesia),

MAP INDEX

St. Peter's cathedral in Rome.

Main entries for subjects are shown in **bold** type.

INDEX

ACKNOWLEDGMENTS

The Publishers would like to thank the following for permission to reproduce their photographs in this book:

AKG London (36 top); British Library (62); Christian Aid/E. Duigenan (77, top); Frank Spooner Pictures/Gamma Press/Bouvet (79, top); Frank Spooner Pictures/Gamma Press/South Light (79, bottom); Alain le Garsmeur/Impact Photos (12); Hulton Deutsch (55; 59; 64; 66, right; 69; 71; 74, left); Mary Evans Picture Library (54; 56; 61); Peter Newark's American Pictures (60); Peter Newark's Pictures (49); Popperfoto (7; 51, top; 66, left; 68, left; 70; 72; 73; 74, right; 75); Dr. Morley Read/Science Photo Library (77, bottom); John Reader/Science Photo Library (6,); Scala (36, bottom); Josiah Wedgwood and Sons Ltd (51, bottom); Weimar Archive (68, right).

Every effort has been made to trace and acknowledge ownership of copyright. The Publishers will be glad to make suitable arrangements with any copyright holder whom it has not been possible to contact.